No part of this publication may be reproduced, stored in a retrieval system, or transmitted in any form or by any means, electronic, mechanical, photocopying, recording, scanning, or otherwise, without the prior written permission of the publisher, except in the case of brief quotations within critical reviews and otherwise as permitted by copyright law.

NOTE: This is a work of fiction. Names, characters, places, and incidents are a product of the author's imagination. Any resemblance to real life is purely coincidental. All characters in this story are 18 or older.

Copyright © 2019, Willow Winters Publishing. All rights reserved.

Don't
Let
Go

Willow Winters
Wall Street Journal & USA Today Bestselling Author

Don't Let Go
The Collection

Seductive. Addictive. Captivating.
The irresistible heroes in these stories have those three features in common.
Some stories are second chance; others are fated love. But every single one of them, you'll crave to the last page.

This is a collection of tales published by Willow Winters but no longer available. These stories touched my heart, but were exclusive at the time so if you didn't snag them then, they were lost to you forever.

I wanted to make sure you could read all of my work and now you can.

Happy reading, xx

The stories available in this collection are:
Infatuation, the first novella in the *USA Today* best-selling bundle, Drawn to Him.
Desires in the Night and **Keeping Secrets**, both shorts published in exclusive bundles with best-selling author Adriana Locke.
Bad Boy Next Door, a novella I wrote years ago that I still often think about. The damaged hero and second chance love in this romance is one I wish I could go back to often. It's the final tale included in this collection for a total of 4 stories not available anywhere else!

Infatuation

Prologue

Lila

The air is frigid and the land barren as I stare straight ahead at the quaint Alaskan island. More than that though, it's hauntingly beautiful. I wrap my hands around the cold metal railing of the boat as it bobs in the water, bringing us closer to the shore.

It's not as cold as I imagined it would be, although the breeze and the cool spray of ocean water send a trail of goosebumps down my arms.

It's hard not to go to the very edge and lean forward, since I want to see everything, but the waves are harsh and unforgiving. And I don't trust my own grip. Chills run along my spine as I step away and sit back on the bench, farther away from the edge of the boat.

I've never been to a place so gorgeous before, and I'd never planned to come here either. I'm only here to interview a man I've never met.

I watch the fog billowing up the trees. The colors are shades of soft blues and grays. The thin clouds let only the faintest bit of light through as the night drifts in. Picture perfect fails to describe the sight right before my eyes.

I have to remind myself that I'll only be here for one week. I need to get this job done and leave this place, but my God, Ketchikan is beautiful.

It's an old town, founded on the beliefs of ancient clans.

Everyone knows everyone on this island.

I spent the entire flight to Seattle looking up details of this place once the internet proved useless in discovering anything at all about Alec Kulls, the man my employer was so eager to interview.

All I know is that his family has a rich history, and wealth that keeps the island independent. There's not much known about the town otherwise, simply because they don't rely on anything but the land itself.

As the fog dips lower, revealing more of the pine trees that seem to sit on the far edge of the ocean, I think I see a man. I blink as my lungs still, depriving me of breath. And just like that, he's gone.

There's no way anyone could be out on the edge of the forest, so close to the ocean. I couldn't have seen what I think I saw.

My eyes search the thick trees over and over, but there's nothing to be found but the dense forest.

It was far off in the distance, but I know I saw him. Out of instinct, I grab the arm of a stranger to urge whoever it is to look with me.

An old man in a thick winter coat gives me a scowl that makes his wrinkles seem even more pronounced.

The wind whips across us and I let go of him, feeling embarrassed and alone. I swallow thickly, turning away and muttering a small apology. That's how I've felt since I landed in Seattle and drove straight to the dock. Alone.

I lick my lips, wrapping my arms around my chest and shaking off this odd feeling spreading through every inch of my body. It's slow, like the very waves that rock the ship.

My eyes flicker to the trees on the mountain. He's vanished.

I can still see him in my memory; I swear he was looking at me, too. Even from so far away, looking so small in the dense brush. I can practically feel his gaze on me even now.

My heart flips in my chest in an odd way. It feels like I should run. It thumps hard at the thought, as if confirming my instincts. But just then the small crew moves about me, preparing to dock.

There's only one way to the island, and it's by boat. *This boat.*

Once I step off this ship, there's no going back.

A tingle travels along my skin and pricks the back of my neck. I stare into the trees as the boat rocks and pushes my body forward and the men hustle to tie the thick ropes to the ship. I can't explain why I know without a doubt that the man really was there, and that he was waiting for me.

Chapter 1

Lila

Every worry is left behind as I step into the pleasant warmth of the bed and breakfast's entrance. All this tension and anxiety must be from lack of sleep. I brush the water from my jacket and wipe off my rubber rain boots on the worn welcome mat. The cabin looks like a quintessential grandmother's home. It's just like the pictures I saw online.

The smell of apples and cinnamon hits me the moment I stop in the foyer. I inhale the comforting scents deeply and listen to the crackling of the fire on the far right. The dim lights and warm glow make every touch in the place feel homey.

I roll my suitcase to the sofa and stop, spotting a crockpot on the entry table and white ceramic mugs next to it.

Hot cider. I know it in an instant. I'm quick to shrug off my jacket, looking behind me as I hang it over my suitcase, searching for the owner. I almost put the jacket on the old sofa; it's a dated floral print, but the throw neatly folded over the back of it looks plush and inviting. My jacket is coated with a thin layer of mist from the light rain outside, so I wouldn't dare put it there.

I look around the corner and see a small dining room with a wooden table and chairs. In the center of the table is a stack of pale blue cloth napkins and a set of white salt and pepper shakers that look like owls. But not a soul is there either.

It's quiet, but welcoming.

The cabin itself is small, and someone must've heard me come in.

I shake off the cold from the outdoors, feeling the soothing heat from the fire and go to the crockpot before searching out anyone. I need something to warm me up. Just a moment to myself while my nerves settle. I've been on edge every minute of this trip. I know part of it is my fear of flying. It's a stupid fear. I've heard every statistic, and I've been told over and over that flying is safe. But I'll be damned if I could breathe for even a second of that six-hour flight.

The heavy smell of cinnamon greets me as I lay the glass lid down on the table and pick up the ladle, pouring a serving and then another into one of the mugs.

I'd give anything to shake this overwhelming apprehension that seems to be clinging to me.

I close my eyes, letting the heat of the cider travel through my chest and the taste of apples and cinnamon tickle my tongue. I smile into the mug, taking another sip before slowly sinking into the sofa and letting the flames of the fire warm me.

I roll my head to the side wanting to ease the tension, but it only makes me that much more tired. Already I'm exhausted from this trip, and it's only just begun.

I wish I could have stayed longer in Seattle. It's absolutely gorgeous, although opposite in beauty to this island. Where Seattle has intricately designed buildings that tower over you and the old streets lined with planted trees and cobblestones, here the nature is untouched. It's not arranged to complement the city structures; the mountains and forests are the sights here. The few houses I saw earlier were tucked back into the thicket and seem to blend in.

That could be due to the hour though. We arrived in the evening as the fog was settling in. Funny how the fog in Seattle seems to dim the city's beauty, but here it only adds to the island's atmosphere.

I take another sip of the cider, watching the flames lick along the logs. My nails click as they tap rhythmically against the mug. Of the two places I've been today, I prefer the island. It has a sense of ancient tradition, the land feeling mostly unsullied.

I grew up in Philadelphia, and seeing the beautiful city of Seattle blew me away. But this remote island is like no other place I've ever been. It calls to me in a way I can't explain.

"Miss Travers?" a small voice calls out from behind me, pulling me from my thoughts. I stand so quickly I nearly spill the cider, feeling embarrassed once again that I've made myself at home and didn't bother seeking anyone out.

"Yes, here," I answer, setting the mug down on the coffee table and turning to face an elderly woman. She pushes a pair of thin-framed glasses up the bridge of her nose as she walks around the back of the sofa to greet me. "Mrs. Joslin?"

"Call me Ada, please," she answers me.

At first I smile and tug my sweater down, ready to get to my room and pass out from the long day, but something in her expression catches me off guard.

There's a smile on her face, but it doesn't reach her eyes and the way she wrings her fingers nervously makes me question the pleasant tone of her voice. "Are you checking in?" she asks.

I find it odd. Obviously I am. What else would I be doing here? I hesitate, trying to remember if today is the first day I booked. I turn halfway, still facing her and trying not to be rude as I lean down to dig inside of my purse for the papers. I fucking hope I didn't screw this up. I don't need to start this trip off by being kicked out of the one bed and breakfast for miles and miles.

"I believe it's today," I say although it comes out sounding like a question.

"Yes, of course," Ada says with confidence and an upbeat lilt that wasn't there before. I peek up at her, the papers in my hands crinkling as I unfold them. They confirm I've booked the entire week; today's date is the first day of my stay.

She tucks her hands into the pockets on the sides of her pale pink flannel pajama shirt and nods. "Do you need help with your bags?" she asks me warmly, but there's a chill to her expression.

"Is everything alright?" I ask her as I shove the papers back into the pocket on the inside of my purse.

"Yes, yes. I just wasn't sure if you'd had a chance to see Mr. Kulls yet?"

"The interview is tomorrow," I reply and she nods slowly. I called before booking and spoke to someone here, possibly Ada, although I don't remember. I wanted to make sure the bed and breakfast was close to the estate. It turns out that it's the only bed and breakfast, so I didn't have much of a choice.

"Am I all set to stay?" I ask her warily.

"Of course, dear, of course," she answers with much more pep in her tone. "Right this way!" she says as she grabs the handle of my suitcase before I can and starts walking off. I look behind me at the mug of cider and then grab my jacket before it falls off my luggage.

For a woman so short she walks quickly, and I have to hastily increase my stride to catch up to her.

"Breakfast will be ready when you are," she says as we pass the small dining room and head down a narrow hallway. The walls are speckled with photographs tucked in a variety of colored and shaped frames. She turns her head to look at me, and my eyes are ripped away from the photo of a young boy and to her gaze instead. "Simply call the number on the phone in your room or come to the front, and I'll have breakfast served for you."

She stops at the last door on the very end and takes out a key, unlocking the door and then handing the key to me. It's an actual key, long and heavy. I think it's made of cast iron, and it catches me by surprise. "If you need anything at all, please don't hesitate to ask," she says and her voice is soft and comforting and the small smile on her face is genuine. Her pale blue eyes are sincere, and I almost second-guess her hesitation in the foyer.

"Thank you, Mrs.- Ada," I say and then peer into the room, taking the handle of my suitcase.

"I'll be right down the hall," she says and then turns to walk off. I watch her for a moment and then let out a heavy sigh. Traveling is meant to be stressful. And that's what I'll chalk this up to.

The sound of the wheels rolling is muted as I drag the suitcase onto the plush cream carpet and close the door with a soft click. I lock it out of habit and then drag the heavy bag to the bed. My purse falls off my shoulder and onto the crook of my arm as I struggle with the damn thing. I stare at the bed and then to the suitcase. There's no way I'm getting it up there.

I don't have the energy for anything other than to slip into my PJ bottoms and a baggy t-shirt. My makeup can just wait till the morning, and brushing my teeth can wait, too.

As I crawl into bed I nearly moan at the thought of sleeping peacefully. I'm finally on land and in a beautiful cabin tucked away on this gorgeous island. I close my eyes and the moment I do, I remember the man from earlier.

My heart stills and my eyes pop open as I pull the

comforter up tighter around me and try to forget. I need to sleep, and that's just what I do. But the vision of the man comes back over and over as I drift to sleep. I can't keep him away although I can't quite see his face or any identifying features at all. Each time there's something different about him or the mountain that makes me question whether or not he was real.

But I dream of him. Of climbing through the forest and standing at the edge.

In my dreams, he was waiting for me. And instead of fear, I only feel... wanted.

Chapter 2

Lila

The morning air in Philadelphia can be at times, stale. Suffocating, even. The sounds of other people are constant, along with car horns and yelling for cabbies. My street, in particular, is busy as it's just beyond the more crowded shopping districts.

This is nothing like that.

I inhale deeply, taking a moment to sway back and forth on the porch swing. Time seems slower here. The toe of my boot drags back and forth as I stare forward, waiting for the car that's coming to pick me up. It's not a cab; they don't have those here. Ada's cousin is happy to see me to the Kulls' estate though. Last night the captain of the ship, Drew, drove me here last night.

I chew the inside of my cheek, wondering if I should tip him. Obviously I should. I didn't tip Drew though, he seemed offended I offered. I shake off the memory of the way he looked at me and take a look around.

I'm definitely not in Philadelphia anymore.

The sound of a critter rustling in the dry leaves behind me makes me pop up and off the swing in an instant. I turn around just in time to watch something run off, my hand on my chest and the chill of the morning breeze traveling through the gap in my jacket. A deer, maybe? I'm not sure. But I let out a small huff of a laugh at how absurd I am. Of course there are animals here. Online it said the population of black bears here is higher than the number of humans.

Just as I turn back to face the gravel dirt road that leads to the cabin, Ada steps out onto the porch. At the same time, an old Chevy pickup truck pulls into the driveway. I watch Ada's face as she cocks a brow in surprise and purses her lips.

The truck comes to a stop, and the sputtering sounds of the engine are silenced. Her cousin, I think she said his name was Brant, opens the faded red door as she walks out to meet him.

I clear my throat, feeling the tension between them as she asks him, "You couldn't bring the car?" in a voice that makes damn sure to display her irritation.

I bend down to pick up my purse; it's heavy as hell, and the thin straps dig into my shoulder. It feels like I've stuffed it with bricks, but it's only my laptop that has it feeling so damn heavy.

I walk slowly down the steps, moving closer to the truck with a smile plastered on my face. I couldn't care less what car we drive in so long as I get to my appointment on time.

The two of them turn to me, stopping mid-conversation which only makes me self-conscious. *Maybe I should have stayed on the porch.*

"It's so pretty out today." I barely get the words out, the strength in my voice diminished by them staring at me. I clear my throat as I feel my smile falter.

Brant looks up and nods his head, patting his keys on his jeans. The plaid coat he's wearing appears rumpled as he shoots me a smile. "Not so bad today. It's gray a lot here, so you got lucky I suppose," he answers in a deep voice.

"You've got everything you want to take?" Ada asks me, but the same look in her eyes from last night is back. All morning things were smooth and easygoing. I thought last night must've been my mistake. That maybe it hadn't been as awkward as I thought it was. But right now, clear as day with a full cup of coffee in me, I can feel something's off.

"I've got everything," I say and nod once, feeling my body tense and my expression change. She must see it too, because the other version of her comes back.

"Have a good trip," she says cheerily and starts to walk back to the porch. "Oh, and interview," she adds with a nod, although her voice is lower and more subdued.

I watch her over my shoulder, shuffling the straps of my bag slightly until Brant slaps his hand down on his truck and asks, "You ready?"

It's awkward. We're sitting in silence. Well, the radio is playing softly, but ever since I got in the cramped back seat of the truck, no small talk has been made. The front seat has no seatbelt, so I'm tucked away in the back, safe and sound. I suppose I could comment on the weather... again.

My purse is next to me, leaning against a toolbox that's definitely seen better days. My boots kick a pair of cleats sitting in the back of the truck as we drive over a hole in the road.

"How long do you think it'll be?" I raise my voice to ask Brant, and his eyes find mine in the rearview.

"Another half hour or so," he answers me. He turns

down the radio and glances at me in the rearview again. "What's the interview about?"

"The island mostly," I reply. Sharon Hartfield, my boss and the editor of The Morning Reads, was adamant I interview Mr. Kulls. But the typical synopsis and agenda were missing. Sharon didn't give me anything to go on other than, "Whatever you can get from him." It makes me nervous. She's been giving me more and more responsibility, but this interview is different from the usual protocol.

"The island," Brant repeats easily, nodding his head and looking over to the left as we come to a red light.

"The views here are amazing," I speak without thinking as my breath is taken away. The small town is old and not quite updated yet, but it doesn't feel as though it's needed. There's an undeniable charm to the aged buildings and traditional touches. What's striking is how it's intermingled with nature, which is also untouched.

I watch a small stream of water flow down the foreboding mountain on my left. Utterly gorgeous. "What about the island?" Brant breaks me from my thoughts as the truck moves forward, bringing us back to the interview. To work.

I clear my throat and pull at my seatbelt. "Well, the island is mostly self-sustaining and I've heard it's due to traditions and in a good part because of the Kulls?" I say although it's really a question. More of a hunch I've gathered.

Brant nods his head slowly, but doesn't speak. Just as my hope of gaining a little intel dies, he says, "The brothers brought back more jobs, a better economy I suppose."

"What do you mean?" I ask.

His hands twist on the wheel as if debating on telling me something. I almost have to press, but after a moment he sighs and says, "His father was different is all."

"Have the Kulls always…" I don't know how to end my question, but I don't have to.

"Everyone here descends from ancient clans. Mostly two. And we followed those traditions, but Alec's father did not. It was more about money than anything else." He huffs in obvious disapproval, but continues. "They already had it all. They're the wealthiest and determine most of what goes on around here."

I reach into my purse as I ask, "What traditions did their father stray from exactly?"

Brant's eyes find mine in the mirror as he answers, "All of them."

My pen clicks in the quiet air as I get out my small notebook. It's leather-bound and filled with scribbled notes. I turn to a clean page and ask, "So the new generation of Kulls, they're bringing back the old traditions?"

When he doesn't answer me, I look up to see Brant smirking as he says, "Not quite."

He doesn't continue, and the look on his face is as though he knows something I don't.

"Could you elaborate?" I ask him.

I watch as his jaw clenches and the truck makes a wide turn onto a cobblestone road. It looks new and clean; unlike the others I've seen so far.

"Some traditions died a long time ago, and their father wanted them all to go. He wanted industry here, and that caused a lot of tension."

"Political tension?' I ask.

Brant clucks his tongue and says, "You could say that."

"I don't see much industry here," I point out. It's true. Everything looks like small mom and pop stores.

"There's some, but not much. In the last couple of decades, the town's focus has been on sustainability and self-reliance."

"Since the sons took over?" I ask him to clarify.

Again he shrugs and says, "It was happening regardless of the Kulls. They have the wealth, but their father's disregard of our ways shook their foothold in the law." I jot down all of these gems of history. Brant continues telling me about their water supplies and electrical systems, although most of that info I saw online. The history of the Kulls that's not exposed yet is more of what I want.

"What happened to his father?" I ask.

He shrugs and the truck turns down a path that's shaded by trees, obviously a driveway. "He grew old," he finally answers, but the sight of the estate takes my immediate attention.

It's grand and intimidating. Old money would best describe it. The once copper roof now has a rich patina in a beautiful shade of pale green. It's the perfect accent for the cream stone and manicured dark green ivy along the side of the house, as if they knew all those years ago when it was built that it would look stunning at this very moment. Besides the ivy, there's no shrubbery in sight, only the pine trees on either side.

"Oh," I manage to get out only that single word as the truck stops in front of the estate. The loud rumbling of the engine seems so out of place here. I glance down at myself, smoothing out my cream silk blouse and taking a steadying breath as I reach for my purse. The second my back is turned, my door opens.

A gasp slips from my lips as my grip tightens on my purse straps. The man staring back at me is as breathtaking as the scenery. His eyes are a pale blue and at complete odds with his dark brown hair. It's so dark, it's nearly black.

"Miss Travers," the man says with a deep voice that echoes through my body and heats my blood. For a moment, I'm stunned from the intensity of his gaze but also from the way he said my name. Like he already knew me. *Like he owns me.*

It's only when he takes a step back that I regain my composure and slowly slip out of the truck. It's high up off the ground and when I look down, the man offers me his hand.

I slip my small palm against his and his fingers wrap around my hand as I take the large step down. The heat between us travels through me instantly. Embarrassingly so.

I quickly retrieve my hand and hold the straps of my purse with both hands, taking a step back, my ass bumping against the truck.

In the confines of the truck, I thought maybe this man was staff or a butler, I'm not sure who, but I didn't expect Alec to be the one opening the truck door for me.

Standing on the edge of the long driveway, staring straight at him, I'm sure it's him. His high cheekbones and the rough stubble along his jaw are just as they were in the photographs online. Alec Kulls. The pictures didn't do him justice in the least.

"Mr. Kulls," I finally get a grip and offer my hand out for a handshake. He takes a moment to look at it, leaving my hand dangling in the cold air before accepting it. And again, the instant he touches me, electricity rips through my body, making my thighs clench and my nipples pebble.

"Nice to meet you," he says, and his low voice makes my heart stutter.

I don't know what's come over me. I rip my hand away again, trying to ignore the tingling prickle at the back of my neck. It's not until Mr. Kulls shakes Brant's hand and the two share a glance that I snap out of it.

"Her bags?" he asks Brant, and the trace of a smile on Alec's lips falls when Brant shakes his head.

Mr. Kulls' eyes narrow and Brant merely shrugs his shoulders, but there's a smirk on Brant's lips that makes me think there's something else between them.

"Thank you so much for having me and agreeing to this interview," I say to Alec with more strength than I realized I had left. As my senses slip back into place, I turn to Brant. "Oh, and thank you so much for the ride," I start to say while I dig for my wallet.

"Don't you dare," Alec says and the tone of his voice makes my blood chill. I hear the slap of two hands meeting and look up to see Brant palming folded up cash.

"My pleasure, Miss Travers." The way Brant says my name seems to be in a mocking tone. But not to me, its focus is on Alec.

"Thank you," I mutter in a small voice, feeling as if there's a joke I'm not aware of, yet somehow a part of.

I watch Brant walk around to the other side of the truck before taking a glance at Alec. "Thank you, I could have paid-"

"Not a problem at all," he cuts me off and when his eyes reach mine again, the corners of his lips seem to tug up slightly.

"Why don't you come in?" The way the words fall from Alec's lips is tempting and seductive in a way I hadn't expected. It's not that he's flirtatious in the least… it's something else.

I take a few steps, following him, my eyes taking in the details of his tailored and clearly expensive suit until he peeks over his shoulder. I feel the heat of a blush rise up my cheeks as he smirks at me, clearly catching me in the act. I part my lips to utter an apology or explanation, but all sense of professionalism seems to have left me. Luckily I'm saved by Mr. Kulls as he opens his door and says, "Let's get this interview started."

Chapter 3

Lila

"I trust you had a sound flight and travels?" Mr. Kulls asks me as he closes the tall front door. Like the rest of the house, it has history; the dark rich walnut was obviously carved by hand.

"I did," I answer politely. "Thank you for asking." I try to remain professional as I take in the the estate. The high ceilings and intricate architecture are magnificent. "And again, thank you for the interview, Mr. Kulls."

"Alec, please," he says, reaching his hand out, and it takes me a moment to realize he's asking for my coat. I'm quick to respond, moving my purse to the floor so I can shrug off the jacket. The cool draft stays with me for a moment, but the home itself is warm and instantly replaces the cold.

"Thank you... Alec," I add his first name, feeling the shy blush creep back onto my cheeks. This is quickly becoming unlike any interview I've done before. And I'm well aware it's because I'm attracted to Alec. I have to remind myself that I'm working. That this is a job and I'm a professional, for fuck's sake.

He gives me a small smile that slowly widens as he hangs my coat on an iron rack to the left of the grand foyer. As if he can't contain his mirth, maybe because he senses the attraction, or maybe because I'm obviously flustered. I'm not sure which.

"This way," he says and starts walking, the sound of his oxford shoes smacking against the granite echoing off the walls.

The inside of the estate is just as stunning as the outside with rich red walls and marble stone floors.

I hurry my steps to catch up to him. "This is your family's estate?" I ask to get my mind back on track. The little pieces of Kulls history Brant gave me were interesting. I could whip up something interesting about companies that have been passed down through generations and stay within families, easily tying this story to a relevant family company back in Philadelphia.

I nod my head and sneak a look to my left at him.

That could be a good spin. Related, yet interesting to compare. Although I'm much shorter than Alec, my strides are in time with his as I follow him down a long corridor past several closed doors and into an office.

Or maybe a library. My Lord. Alec stops behind a large oak desk covered with stacks of papers, devoid of a computer or any technology at all. Behind him are a set of three large windows, the towering mountains and pine trees making it seem as though they're paintings and not a vista of the outdoors. The telling sign that it's the actual view is the snow that's started falling and sweeping across the sky in the breeze.

My purse slowly slips from my shoulder and lands with a thud on the intricate, darkly colored, handwoven rug. The walls to my left and right are lined with bookshelves and what must be thousands of books.

My lips part, my mouth hanging open, but I don't even know where to begin.

"You're out of your element, Miss Travers?" Alec's voice caresses my consciousness, and I dare to look him in the eyes.

"I am," I tell him honestly. I've worked for Sharon for three years now, assigned an interview every other week or so. I've been blown away a few times, but nothing like this.

His lips twitch again, although he keeps the smile at bay. "Please, have a seat. Unless you'd like to explore first?" He cocks a brow, waiting for my response and gesturing to the shelves of books.

I shake my head with a tight smile and pull my blouse down so that it covers the tight black leggings to nearly my knees.

"Tea first?" Alec offers as I settle into the leather seat, my hands gripping the carved armrests. "No, thank you," I reply as he pours a cup on the other side of the desk. I watch as the steam rises, and the soft sound of the tea spilling into the cup is soothing. The clink of the porcelain cup hitting the saucer almost makes me wish I'd said yes.

My brown boots come up mid-thigh and brush against one another as I cross my legs. "May I have a look around once the interview is over? I'm curious to see the estate."

Alec nods once and walks around the desk to take the seat next to me, surprising me. I clear my throat and angle the chair to face him just as he does.

"Of course," he says, leaning back with his right ankle on his left knee and his hands clasped in his lap. "Whenever you'd like."

"Thank you," I tell him as I bend down and pick up my notebook and pen. "I really appreciate it."

"No recorder?" he asks and I shake my head. I flip through the pages and find where I left off with Brant, making a clean line and writing Alec's initials where the break starts. "I prefer this way," I explain.

"Alright then... Lila." He says my name as if it's a way to tease me. I raise my eyes to him, the pen still on the notepad. "What would you like to know?"

With his father in mind, I ask a question I hope will put him at ease and allow me to uncover new details about the Kulls. "Your business is family-run from what I've read?"

He nods his head once, running his thumb along the tips of his fingers. "Myself and my two brothers, Marcus and Elliot."

I scribble their names down and ask, "And before you three, did your father run it with his siblings or was he an only child?"

"My father did everything on his own. He was an only child and alone most of his life."

I lift my head to look into his eyes as I say, "Alone?" Alec only nods in response.

My back settles against the leather as I give him a small smile and ask, "Could I take you up on that offer for tea, Mr. Kulls?" My voice is soft and sweet.

He smirks at me, rising from his seat, but not answering me. As he pours the tea I watch the snow falling behind him, covering the already white ground.

"You don't have to coax me, Lila," Alec says, placing

the cup on the saucer and bringing it to me. "I'm happy to address whatever it is that's on your mind."

Goosebumps flow down my arms. *Caught in the act.* "Was I that obvious?" I ask him, not willing to hide the fact that yes, I was playing into his ego to get him in a favorable mood.

"What do you really want to know?" he asks, passing me the tea.

I swallow thickly, taking the hot cup and watching as he retakes his seat. The steam drifts up and begs me to take a sip. I lift the cup to my lips, but I don't drink just yet. "Brant, the driver," I start to explain, not sure if he knows who I'm talking about.

"I know who Brant is. Just spit it out," he says with his fingers steepled and the tips tapping against one another.

Although I appreciate his no-nonsense attitude, I'm intimidated, but I won't shy away. "Brant mentioned that your father broke tradition?" I say as I glance back down to my notes. Alec gives me a look of confusion at first and then lets out a heavy sigh as his eyes flash with a knowing look.

"That's not very fair of Brant. It wasn't just my father." Alec looks over his shoulder and out of the window and then back at me. "You want to hear the history of the town?" He gestures behind him to the shelves and shelves of books as I nod. "I've got plenty of books that will tell you the ins and outs of the economy and where our money comes from. The names of those who took office and how the laws changed over time. There are even books on heritage and marriages."

I purse my lips, nearly ready to tell him that I want to hear about only *his* father and their family's history, but he continues.

"You'll find the Kulls have been influential since as far back as we can date. The history of the island starts with my family, and we've maintained our position throughout generations."

"What position is that? You don't hold offices."

"There's a small sheriff here and elected officials, but they hold positions to fill in seats and make sure things run smoothly. The Kulls maintain wealth, not only monetary, but also land and the decisions to invest in certain industries have been critical to our island's economy."

"So, you provide the jobs?"

Alec shakes his head. "Not exactly. More like we make sure there are jobs available, because we make sure the resources are already here before they're needed. As a result, the money on the island doesn't have to go overseas. The estate holds a huge stake in the natural resources here. If anything runs low, we acquire and disperse it as needed."

I can feel my eyes narrowing, but before I can ask anything further, he adds, "In the last two decades, we've ensured that the island can sustain the three-hundred-person population on its own. With modern technology, access to anything a person can desire is available through the shipping ports. This town likes to keep its traditions, to stay independent and maintain a relatively hidden and quiet lifestyle. We make certain it's possible."

I take a moment to write the information down, but it's not what I wanted to discuss. This is simply business jargon. It'd make for an interesting piece maybe, but one question pops out at me. "What's in it for you?"

"This is simply what the Kulls do, and of course the income and notoriety are a bonus," he says as he taps his pointer finger to his lip. "That's not quite what you were after, is it?" he asks me after a moment.

"It's not," I tell him honestly.

"What then?" he asks, leaning forward with his elbows on his knees.

"What *traditions* were left behind?" I ask Alec, and he shakes his head as he sits back in his chair.

His eyes search my face for something, but I'm not sure what though. Finally, he answers, "The island descends from ancient clans who took pride in nature and made every decision based on customs and folklore."

He licks his lips, and my eyes are drawn to them. "Even marriages were determined by old traditions, up until my grandfather's generation." I nod, and he continues.

"Although the island fell out of the old ways with the industrial revolution, some beliefs still carry on to this day."

"Which ones?"

A huff of a laugh leaves him as he says, "Ones my father refused to teach us, I'm afraid."

"Why's that?"

He noticeably swallows and for the first time he seems uncomfortable, but before I can take it back, he speaks. He looks past me at the books behind me as he talks. "He married my mother according to what he was supposed to do, and she passed away giving birth to my youngest brother, Elliot. They were only together for twelve short years."

"I'm so sorry," I say and he waves off my apology, continuing.

"He wasn't supposed to remarry. The elders wouldn't bless a second marriage. They're all gone now with no one left to replace them, because my father made sure of that. Back then, everyone took their word as law. They said my mother was the only one meant for him, and that if he remarried it would be an atrocity and place shame on our family."

Alec gives me a sad smile as he continues. "He

demanded the ritual regardless. It involves a tincture for those who haven't found their partner. The tales say that once you've had a taste of it, within a day's end you'll have found the one you're meant to be with."

"A tincture?" I ask, cocking a brow and shifting my legs to get more comfortable. The tea cup rattles in my lap as Alec nods his head and continues. It's almost a fairytale-like story. Or maybe something darker, but this is what I want to hear. Even if the article ends up being paragraphs about business, shipping docks and sustainability, I'd rather spend hours listening to tales like this.

"My father said the elders lied, and that he'd found his new wife the very next day after drinking the concoction. When she died only a few months into their marriage, it hit my father hard."

"How old were you?" I ask him cautiously.

"I was only seven. Elliot was six, and my brother Marcus was twelve."

"And then the three of you took over the company years later. Because he'd passed away?"

Alec nods. "For ten years, things took a turn for the worse, for both our family and the island, but we recovered. A decade and a half later, and all has been salvaged."

"Do you believe your father?" I ask him.

He grins at me, a devilish look that makes me question my naivety. "My brothers and I didn't get this company back on top with tradition and folklore."

My eyes fall and I feel foolish until he adds, "Three months ago, I went with my brother Marcus, and we bought the mix from the old women on the far side of the mountain. They live by the land there and still carry on the old traditions."

"Why did you go there?"

Alec taps his fingers against his knee as he answers, "Marcus is older than me, and all three of us have lived relatively solitary lives." His gaze wavers for a moment, a sadness coating his voice as he adds, "Marcus wanted a wife. He wanted someone to love. So we went there for the tincture, the very same one my father claimed worked for him."

"You drank the tincture?" I ask to clarify.

"I did." He nods as he answers me.

"And?" I can't help but ask, "Did you meet your soul mate?" I try to add a note of humor to my voice, realizing how foolish the notion is, but the romantic heart in me is beating slowly, waiting for an answer with bated breath.

"My brother went out searching for his. He's desperate for someone in his life. I only drank it to prove a point to him." The coldness in his voice catches me off guard, and something in his tone makes my heart clench with nearly unbearable pain. "I stayed in this room for the next day and a half." He holds my gaze as he adds, "I didn't see a soul."

My blood turns to ice and I look down at my notepad trying to take a few steps back, but I feel lost and emotional. His story made me feel hopeful, alive. Like how I used to get when I was a child reading Disney books.

"All I did was read," he says in a tone that sounds sympathetic and comforting; like he senses this upsets me and wishes it didn't.

I clear my throat and stare past him as he says, "The time has gotten away from me." He stands, and I finally notice the snow hasn't stopped falling. There's not a spot remaining which isn't blanketed beneath a thick layer of snow.

"You can stay here tonight," Alec says with no room for negotiation in his tone. "The mountain isn't safe for traveling."

Chapter 4

Lila

"I really don't want to put you out." I stare out of the window in the kitchen. The ground is still carpeted with several feet of snow, but it's practically raining now. "I think-"

"Brant's not going to be able to make it up the mountain safely with the hail," Alec says confidently, cutting off any excuse that I have. I open my mouth to protest, but he turns to me with his brows raised.

"Don't worry, Lila," he says with a small smile. "It happens from time to time here." His eyes flicker to me and then back to the chicken on the cutting board.

I don't know how an interview turned into having a

sexy stranger cooking for me. It feels like a date in every possible way.

"It doesn't where I'm from," I say uneasily, looking outside. The bay window has a small seat attached. It's so out of place in the updated and masculine kitchen.

The seat itself looks it should be littered with pillows and have a small shelf of books next to it. It's a tempting reading nook, just outside of the kitchen and a few feet from the dining room table. I could see myself sitting there and writing.

"Would you like a seat?" Alec asks as he catches me staring at the window seat.

"Oh, no, I'm fine here," I say. Tucking a stray lock of hair behind my ear, I try to shake off this awkward feeling, but it won't go away.

"Relax," Alec says, setting down the knife and walking to the sink. He washes his hands as he talks over the sound of the faucet running. "As you can imagine, snow-ins aren't so uncommon here," he tells me.

I watch his broad shoulders move as he dries his hands off and checks the thermometer of the oven. As he does, the beep goes off letting him know it's up to temperature.

"I'm sorry," I tell him. It's so obvious I'm uncomfortable, and I don't want him to think I'm ungrateful.

He picks up a cherry tomato from the small pile on

the counter and tosses it into his mouth, turning to face me and leaning against the island.

"I understand this is different and I have to confess, I'm partially to blame."

My eyes whip up to his, and I'm not sure how to respond.

"To blame?" I echo. My blood heats with the way he looks at me.

"I may have requested that you be the one to come here," he says and then reaches over and takes another cherry tomato between his fingers. He holds my gaze as he pops it into his mouth. The action is sensual in a way, but threatening as well.

I take a breath, trying to keep it even. Trying not to let what he's just admitted affect me.

As if reading my mind, Alec smiles, chewing and swallowing the tomato slowly with his hands raised in the air. When he's finished with it he lets out a small laugh that lightens the mood. "Maybe I shouldn't have told you that." His eyes sparkle with something they haven't before, an easiness and humor that make him seem less dominating and intimidating. "I just wanted you to know that I hadn't planned on this," he gestures to the window. "But I did want to meet you," he adds as he cocks a brow at me and then turns to the counter, moving the chicken to a tray and slipping it into the oven.

"I read a few of your articles. You're a talented writer, and you're attractive. You can't blame me for wanting you to be the one to conduct the interview," he says, closing the oven door. He turns to me and adds, "Maybe I could even take you on a date?" He raises his hands again, palms out and says, "No pressure. I just thought you may enjoy seeing the town and taking a tour."

"We're snowed in," I answer him with the obvious response, not sure how to react to this man.

My body is on fire at the thought of him wanting me. Just the fact he's interested in me is driving adrenaline through my blood. At the same time, I'm easy prey for him. Someone for him to use up and spit out. I'm practically trapped in his home. I take in a heavy breath, hating how the last thought somehow makes me even hotter.

"Not tonight, but perhaps tomorrow if the weather lets up?" He takes a few steps closer to me.

"I would enjoy that," I answer politely and then grip the back of the island chair and pull it out so I can take a seat.

"You just need to relax, Lila," Alec says as he walks over to a carved cherry liquor cabinet, pulling out two bottles of wine, one red and the other white. "Usually I would have white, considering the meat," he says, reading the labels of each bottle before peeking up at me. "But which would you prefer?"

"Whichever you'd like," I answer, not really caring which one he'll choose. The tables have turned, and as my fingers twine around one another I have to remind myself that I'm leaving in a few days. That this isn't really a date. Although it damn sure feels like it, and he's said he's interested in me.

It would be a mistake. I watch as he grabs a bottle opener. *A beautiful mistake.*

He opens the bottle of white easily, pouring one glass and then another. They clink together as he picks them up in one hand and takes the seat next to me.

He places the glasses down on the counter and passes mine to me, simply sliding it across the counter as if it's an offering. I can't help but let out a small laugh. He smiles in response, a handsome smile that makes my fingers itch to touch the stubble along his jaw.

"You're very handsome, Mr. Kulls." I finally give in to a bit of my desire, and pick up the glass of wine, holding on to it for support in this decision.

His grin widens and he leans forward just slightly to say, "Alec, Lila. My name is Alec to you." He pauses for a moment, then flashes me a smirk and adds, "Unless of course you'd like to scream 'Mr. Kulls' in bed?"

My face heats instantly as he rises from his seat to attend to the beeping oven and he's quick to say, "I do believe Alec may be easier."

The sweet wine touches my lips and the taste is delicious, but I can't think of anything other than this man on top of me, making me scream as he thrusts inside of me repeatedly.

"I think you've maybe thought a little too far ahead, Mr.- Alec," I'm quick to correct myself. I watch as he works in the oven, turning the chicken breasts and then setting the tongs back down on the counter before coming back to his seat.

"Mmm, that could be," he says picking up his glass, but not sitting. I cross my ankles and turn in my seat to face him.

"This isn't very professional," I tell him with a serious look, or at least the most serious I can manage. He shrugs his shoulders and then takes a sip from his glass.

"Do you want it to be?" he asks and then adds, "That's fine if you do. I understand the attraction may only be on my end."

My heart thumps hard in my chest. I don't think this man knows how to be subtle. He's honest and to the point. But I admire that.

"It's definitely not just one-sided," I admit, and then bite my tongue. I'm thinking I should add that this is dangerous for me. I could lose my job. More than that though, this man could crush me. I've never had a one-night stand because I know I don't really do casual. I've been wined and dined and then thrown away before. It hurts too much.

I don't recover easily, and I prefer to avoid relationships. But it's been so long since I've been touched.

Alec's deep voice rumbles, "That's good to know." I don't think a man has ever looked at me with the same level of desire. It's tempting and frightening all the same.

"So, tomorrow?" he asks me, and my brow furrows with confusion.

"Tomorrow?" I repeat.

He smiles at me, and the smell of his cologne, or maybe his natural scent hits me with a powerful force that makes me lean in closer to him.

"Would you like to go out with me tomorrow?" he asks.

His gray eyes swirl with a mixture of desire and something else--a desperate need. I nod my head slowly and say, "I'd love to."

Chapter 5

Lila

My eyes pop open as I hear Alec in the kitchen. My bare feet pad on the wooden stairs and I clutch his white dress shirt I'm wearing tighter. *His*. I'm fucking mortified.

I hardly slept, even with a stomach full of hot food and delicious wine. I was *this* close to sleeping with Alec, to kissing him and making a fool of myself last night. I don't know what came over me.

Nothing has been normal about the last two days.

And I don't know what to expect today. Or where to find my clothes. We didn't have sex; I know that much. I'm fairly sure I asked for a dress shirt to sleep in. *Specifically, a dress shirt, because that's an obvious choice to sleep in.*

I roll my eyes and try not to groan at the thought. This is worse than a walk of shame. I didn't even get to have sex.

As I turn the corner headed toward the kitchen, I spot my suitcase in an instant. The faded blue and bulky casing stands out like a sore thumb on the window seat.

I cast a furtive glance at Alec, hoping I can sneak in and grab it, but it's no use. He looks up at me from his laptop and says easily, "Good morning."

My grip on the dress shirt tightens as I try to swallow.

"Morning," I mutter and glance at my suitcase, desperate to change and try to collect myself.

"Drew brought it over this morning." Alec closes the laptop and leans back in his seat, his eyes assessing me. "I thought about bringing it up to you, but I didn't want to wake you."

My throat's tight as I answer, "Thank you."

"How did you sleep?" he asks. I wonder if this is normal for him, to have random women in his clothes parading through his house half-naked on the weekends.

The thought makes me angry and fuels me to walk toward my suitcase.

Last night was a mistake.

"Fine, thank you," I answer him brusquely although I can't look him in the eyes. I stop when he asks me, "Is something wrong?"

"Just feeling out of sorts." I hope he'll just accept it and let me go about my way. I'm a fool for getting drunk last night.

"Do you need help with that?" he offers and rises from his seat.

I shake my head so fast that my hair swishes against my shoulders.

"Are you being shy?" he asks me, walking around the counter to a coffee maker. The sight is instantly accompanied by the smell of coffee, and that alone is enough to tempt me to stay just a bit longer.

Shy? Not quite the right word. I clear my throat. "Just a bit embarrassed about last night," I admit, feeling anxiety creep through me.

"Nothing to be embarrassed about," Alec says as he takes a mug out and pours a cup of black coffee. I note that he doesn't add either creamer or sugar as he takes a sip.

He stares at the coffee and then across the room to look at me as he says, "I enjoyed last night."

The way he says it makes me question if we did have sex. We didn't though. I distinctly remember coming on to him and being denied.

I hesitate to come up with a response, and he smiles at my frustration. "It was fun having someone to talk to. I really enjoy your company, Lila," he says with his voice full of sincerity.

I nod my head once. "It was... fun," I finally say.

A deep rough chuckle fills the room. "Is that why you seem to be in a hurry to leave?" he asks, and it makes me feel like shit. I don't want to be obvious, but really, what did he expect? Maybe it would have been different had I woken up in his bed in the morning, but then again, it probably would have made me feel even more like shit.

"I just don't do this," I say and gesture between us.

"I don't either," he's quick to reply and then takes another sip of his coffee. He gives me a tight smile as he says, "You're the first person to stay here since my brother's left."

His admission catches me off guard. I'm not that naïve. I narrow my eyes at him, but he only shakes his head. "I wouldn't lie, Lila." He reaches into the cabinet, turning away from me and picking up a mug. The ceramic clinks against another cup before he sets it down on the counter.

"Would you like a cup? Maybe some coffee and a hot shower will have you feeling better?" he offers.

The thought of both a hot shower and fresh cup of coffee makes me relax almost instantly.

Yes, that's just what I need. "Please," I answer and walk toward the island. I'm acutely aware I'm only in Alec's dress shirt and my underwear, but he doesn't seem to mind in the least. His reaction is surprising, in the best of ways. "When I came down here, I wasn't sure what to expect," I tell him and watch for his response.

"And?" he asks me.

"And what?"

"Are you happy I hadn't run off?" he asks with a smile and then brings the cup to me. "Sugar?" he asks. I stare at him from across the counter.

"You don't have to do this," I tell him simply. "You don't need to cater to me and do all of this-"

"Do you think I don't want to?" he cuts me off, not bothering to wait for me to answer that yes, I do like sugar and creamer. Instead he goes about fetching both, setting them on the counter opposite me. "I'm not doing anything I don't want to, Lila." His brow creases as he looks back at me. "Like I said, I enjoy your company and there's certainly nothing wrong with me being accommodating for a guest."

"Thank you," I whisper, giving in and trying to show my gratitude.

"You're skeptical, and it's because I'm attracted to you," he tells me as I spoon out a large heap of raw sugar and dump it into the steaming mug. I nod my head once, my eyebrows rising.

"Yes," I say and look him in the eyes. "You just want to get into my pants?" It was meant to be a statement, but it turned into a question.

He smirks at me. "If that was the case, we'd still be in bed, Miss Travers."

I glance down at a dark gray swirl in the granite countertop and then back up to him, picking up the small porcelain pitcher of creamer and watching it lighten the dark coffee. "Why is it that we aren't?" I ask him slowly and carefully, dreading the answer.

When I look up at him, I find him looking at me with pure unadulterated pleasure. As if I'm the most amusing thing he's ever seen.

"What's so funny?" I ask, feeling a small smile pulling my lips up simply in response to him.

"You're cute," he says and that smile gets bigger. I shake my head and take a sip of the coffee. It smells rich, tastes delicious and the warmth is desperately needed. It's heaven.

"You make me nervous," I tell him as I put the mug down.

"You're less nervous when you're drunk," he tells me and then lays his forearms on the counter, leaning closer to me. "But I didn't want to take you to bed and have you not remember it."

I nod and feel my cheeks flame, casting my eyes down.

"You did promise me a date last night," Alec says as he pushes away from the counter and out of my reach, the movement catching my attention.

"Did you really bring me out here..." I start to ask and then have to trail off as my head pounds with a morning headache from caffeine withdrawal or maybe a hangover. I grip the mug with both hands. "Did you bring me out here simply because you wanted to sleep with me?" I can't help but ask him the annoying thought that's been bugging me.

Alec scratches the back of his head, looking away from me for a moment. "I shouldn't have said that last night," he starts, and I have to cut him off.

"Are you saying you should have lied?" I ask. I don't know why I'm feeling so defensive, or so much like I want to run.

"I'm saying, your editor contacted me and I requested you. I looked into the others, but I admired your writing and found you attractive," he says easily, the tension in the air dissipating. "It doesn't hurt that I've been alone for a long time and the thought of taking you on a date after the interview... well, I couldn't say no to that."

"Our interview isn't over," I say, trying to remember if I even started a write-up last night. I'm confused with which direction to take the article. Do I go with something that will sell but still be business-oriented that my editor will find appropriate? Or should I stick to what I really want to write?

"First dates are interviews, Lila. And ours went great last night," Alec says with his eyes on me as he raises the mug of coffee to his lips. There's a challenge in his gaze, and I play along.

"Last night was *not* a date." The strength in my voice is gone, and I have to bite down on my lip to keep from smiling.

He doesn't hold back his own as he sets down the mug and swallows. My eyes are drawn to his neck and then up to his lips as he licks them.

"If that's the way you want to play this, that's fine. I'd love to have another *non-date* with you tonight, Miss Travers. But first, an interview over coffee and brunch in town."

"Just an interview?" I ask him, feeling disappointed although I've brought this on myself.

He closes the space between us with his large strides. He gets near enough to where I can touch him if I want, near enough to where he could lean down and put his lips on mine. But neither of those things happens. Instead he leans against the counter and merely stares down at me. The heat crackling between us begs me to initiate something. I refuse it though, gripping my coffee mug and pretending the sexual tension doesn't exist.

"It was never just an interview," he says just above a murmur and the way he says it makes me more than certain those words are the absolute truth. He leans forward, his lips close to my ear, his hot breath trailing down my shoulder and he whispers, "Shower first, and then our date."

Chapter 6

Lila

I suppose it's only natural that Alec takes me to a quaint diner. It's a small town, and it makes sense we'd have an early brunch in a corner booth on the far end of a mom and pop shop.

And maybe it makes sense that everyone keeps giving us odd glances, too. I'm new, and unfamiliar. But constantly feeling their gazes makes me uneasy. I keep glancing between the dark blue paisley window covers and the small crowd on the other side of the diner. Each time there's someone staring back. It's almost like a game at this point.

"Are they bothering you?" Alec asks me, bringing me

out of my thoughts.

I shake my head, both hands wrapped around the white ceramic mug in my hands. Tea this time, not coffee. I limit myself to two cups a day for the sake of my teeth. Coffee's worse than smoking for your teeth, or so I've heard. "I'm just not used to..." I pause and take a moment, trying to come up with the right word. "Attention."

I can still taste the sugary icing from the honey bun I practically devoured. I have a sweet tooth that this diner could certainly satisfy, and I keep eyeing the bit of icing left on the plate sitting on the edge of the table.

Alec nods his head, looking down at the cup of black coffee he hasn't touched since the waitress set it down. "It may have been a mistake to come here," Alec murmurs as he looks past me for a moment.

"Oh?" I chew the inside of my lip, letting my nerves get the best of me. I feel like I'm walking on the edge with this man, teeter-tottering between falling for him and keeping myself guarded. I'm not sure which way I'll fall, but either way, I know I'm going to land hard on my ass.

Alec leans forward, resting his forearms against the pale blue tablecloth and says in a hushed voice, "They're watching us to see who you are to me." His piercing gaze holds me steady as his words register. The small chatter and clinking of utensils turns to white noise.

"Who I am?" I ask him as my heart seems to slow,

each beat hurting just slightly. Just enough to notice it.

I look down at my cup and lift the tea bag up with my spoon and then lower it back down, letting the dark tea mix with the hot water. "Who would that be?" I ask him although another question rests right on the tip of my tongue.

"A good girl who deserves more than a man like me," he says without missing a beat.

I search his eyes, wondering why he said that. "Are you a bad man?" The words slip out without my consent. The moment they leave my lips, I want to snatch them back to keep Alec from hearing, but they're already gone.

He doesn't flinch like I thought he would. He doesn't seem shocked at all by my question. And maybe that's more alarming than anything else.

"My father was," Alec says, not breaking my gaze. "And recently there was an incident with my brother."

His expression reflects pain at the mention of his brother. His light eyes smolder, and his lips turn down.

"Did you hurt him?" I ask. I hardly know Alec, but I can sense a darkness in him. More out of pain than anything else. But it's there, just beneath the surface. It's in the way he carries himself. Even the way he speaks.

Alec shakes his head and says, "Never." He taps his fingers against the mug, and I look up past him at a woman in the very back. She's staring at us shamelessly, and I hate it.

"My brother's a good man. He's nothing like my father." His voice holds conviction, and I find myself confused.

"What then?"

"Do you remember how I told you about the tincture? How I drank it to prove to my brother that it was pointless?" he asks me, and the reminder makes my heart flicker with pain. As if it splinters.

I simply nod and pick up the tea cup, holding it closer, but not drinking.

"He found someone that day, and their relationship is questionable," he says.

Immediately my defenses rise as I blurt out, "It's no one else's business." Anger brims just beneath the surface. "No one has a right to judge a relationship-"

Alec cuts me off by saying, "Even I question it, Lila." I'm silenced and stunned by his admission. "I'm not sure she wants to..." He trails off and runs his hand through his hair, the air turning uncomfortable. "I'm not sure she's interested in being with him as much as he is her," Alec explains, and that definitely changes things.

My eyes catch a glimpse of a man turning to look over his shoulder at us. He's quick to look away, but it's then that everything makes sense. Small towns and gossip go hand in hand.

"Did your brother hurt her?" I ask softly, chancing a glance at him.

His expression hardens, but he hesitates to answer. "She said no and he did as well, but…" He pauses and clears his throat, readjusting in his seat. "It doesn't look good from the outside," he finally says.

"What does it look like from the outside?" I ask.

His expression hardens and he mutters, "Like she's going to leave him." He blows on his coffee and takes a drink before adding, "It'll destroy him if she…" Alec doesn't finish, shrugging his shoulders and setting the coffee mug down.

My fingers trail down the hot ceramic and then I lift it to my lips as Alec tells me, "I haven't talked to anyone about it."

"About your brother?" I ask.

He nods. "It's been difficult to handle because I don't know how to help," he admits, and my instinct is to reach my hand out to him. He huffs a sad laugh, putting his large hand over mine and squeezing it lightly.

"This is too much, isn't it?" he asks me with that sadness reflected in his eyes. "I haven't even known you for twenty-four hours, yet I've told you more personal things than I've told anyone else really." He lets go of my hand to take a sip of his coffee.

"Why me?" I feel compelled to ask.

"I don't know," he says after a long moment. "Maybe it's just the situation." He pulls his hand away, nestling his back against the booth and I miss the warmth of his hand instantly. "I feel helpless about my brother. I'm alone for the first time in a very long time, and I'm only just now realizing how empty my life has been." His confession makes my face crumple.

He gives me that sad smile again. "Being quiet and holding it in hasn't worked well for me. When I saw you," he says and his eyes burn into me, "I felt like you would understand somehow. Or at least that you would keep my secrets."

"Maybe you feel safe with me because I'm leaving," I offer and when I do, his expression changes. He straightens his shoulders, and it's obvious he doesn't like what I've said. "I mean that I'm not a threat to you in any way." I try to lighten the weight of my words as he recoils right in front of me.

"You have no idea how much you threaten me. You make me feel weak, Lila."

Every inch of my skin tingles with awareness. I lick my lips as his eyes heat.

I can't breathe; I can't even react. Just two weeks ago I was on the other side of the country, completely oblivious to this man's existence.

He runs his hands through his hair again and turns

to his left, looking out of his window. "I'm sorry," he says before turning to look me in the eyes and adding, "I know it must sound crazy."

"Someone asked me once if I believed in love at first sight," I say without thinking, just speaking what's on my mind. "I told them no, but I was lying."

Alec huffs a small laugh, and it makes me smile. "Not that I'm saying it's love, because it could be lust," I say.

"There's definitely lust," Alec says in a low tone that vibrates through my body. My chest and cheeks warm and I take a sip of the lukewarm tea, feeling a mix of emotions. I keep thinking back to the tincture. How Alec drank it, how he stayed in a room all day and refused to see anyone. Maybe he delayed it? It's naïve and childish to think of potions and magic, or rituals and séances. Those things don't exist in real life.

I shake off the feeling and my eyes catch sight of a young girl staring at us. Her mother's hand is on her shoulder and everyone else turns away when my gaze reaches them, but not the young girl.

I smile back at her and lift my hand to wave. With the motion, Alec looks behind him, and as the girl waves back he hesitates, but waves as well.

"You're cute," I tell him as I reach into my purse for my wallet.

"First, that's my line. Second, don't you even think

about paying." He reaches into his back pocket and pulls out his wallet before I can reach mine at the bottom of my bag.

"Well, thank you; it was going to be a business expense though."

"I think business is over, Lila," Alec says with a look in his eyes that strums my desire to life. "We should get out of here."

Chapter 7

Lila

"I should go back to the cabin," I tell Alec, but I don't mean it. Every bit of me, down to my very soul, feels for him. In such a short period, he's opened up to me, confided in me. He needs someone so desperately.

We drive in comfortable silence. Maybe he's thinking the same as me. *Where is this going? What are we doing? How will this end?*

The moment we stepped into his warm foyer and out of the cold, the questions seemed to fall silent, replaced by a desire I can't contain.

I slip off my coat slowly, not looking at him, but watching in my periphery as he locks the front door.

"You should…" Alec starts to say as he tosses the keys onto the front entry table. "You definitely shouldn't come upstairs with me," he concludes as he takes two steps closer to me. He stops a foot away, but the proximity is suffocating.

"That would be bad, wouldn't it?" I ask him, although it's not really a question. It's definitely a bad idea to give in to him. To set myself up knowing I'm going to fall hard for him.

My heart begs me to question him. To ask him what he'll think of me after, and try to plan how this could possibly work.

But the moment my lips part, his large hands grip my thighs and pull me up into his arms. I slam into his chest, our lips crashing together and he steals the words from my lips with a hurried kiss. As if letting one more second pass would have killed him.

My chest rises and falls as my fingers spear through his hair while he carries me up the stairs.

As soon as I break the kiss, Alec's lips move to my neck, his hands squeezing my ass as he kicks open a door.

I should say no, but I have no intention of depriving myself of this man.

I want him. It's that easy.

A gasp leaves me as he tosses me onto a large bed. The room is dark with the thick curtains shut, but it's warm and the bed is soft and welcoming.

My eyes are transfixed on Alec as he quickly pulls his shirt over his head, leaving it to fall into a puddle of fabric at his feet. My lips part, and my breathing quickens. My pussy is hot as my thighs clench of their own accord.

I lick my lips as his muscles ripple in the dim light, accenting each hard line. My fingers dig into the comforter, gripping the fabric with the need to keep me right here. His light gray eyes, filled with nothing but desire, hold my own as he unbuttons his pants, shoving them down in a swift push and unleashing his hard as steel cock.

Fuck.

I'm fully clothed, and the man in front of me is naked and gloriously so as he crawls across the bed to get closer to me.

I don't have enough time to admire him, or to think even. My mind is a mess of thoughts, but the overriding one is to give in to every urge and let this man have me however he wants.

"I need," I clear my throat, suddenly feeling shy as he settles between my thighs and unbuttons my jeans.

"What?" he asks me, leaning forward and sneaking in a kiss. I lean into it, but he pulls away and then reaches down, gripping my shirt in his hands and pulling it over my head.

"I'm... I need," I stammer and then just close my eyes

to spit it out. "Birth control."

He laughs, his hot breath sending goosebumps over my body as he buries his head in the crook of my neck. "I'll send for some in the morning. The morning after pill?" he asks, finally leaning away so he can look me in the eye with his brows raised.

I push him playfully on his shoulder. "This is so embarrassing," I huff in a whisper.

Alec doesn't seem to hear me, or if he does, he doesn't care. I fall to the bed and reach behind me, unclasping my bra, preparing to show myself to him.

He doesn't hesitate to pull the straps down and rip the lingerie away, tossing it carelessly to the floor.

I don't have a second to let my self-consciousness show; he immediately leans forward and moans as he sucks my pebbled nipple. His teeth scrape along the sensitive nub, and I beg him to fuck me.

"Please, Alec," I whimper and it's only then that he lets my breast go with a pop of his mouth. He picks my body up in his arms as though it's easy, kicking the covers down and laying me higher up.

It hits me then that this is really happening.

His fingers slide up my thighs slowly and tug my jeans and panties off easily. The rough denim sliding down my skin only makes the pleasure more intense.

Alec pushes my clothes to the side of the bed, and

moves his hand to my pussy. His fingertips slide along my slick sex, and my head lolls back with the faintest touch of pleasure. My clit's already swollen with need and begging for the same attention.

"Fuck," he says with his eyes wide and staring right at me. "You're so fucking wet and ready for me." I can't breathe, and my body's still as he sucks my arousal from his fingertips before moving them back down and pushing two thick fingers into me without hesitation.

My back bows and my body begs me to turn and move away as he finger fucks me, stroking along my front wall. His other hand grabs my throat and pins me down.

My hands instinctively fly to his wrist and fingers around my neck. His grip's not tight or threatening, but the way he plays my body is too intense.

It's like he owns me. Like he could do whatever he wants to me.

And in this moment, he could.

He repositions his hand so his palm smacks against my clit over and over, and the sounds plus the look in his eyes push me over the edge nearly immediately.

A strangled moan and my nails scraping along his wrist and forearm are the only signs he needs that I've come undone. I struggle to catch my breath as he pushes my thighs wider and lines his dick up.

Fuck, he's too big. I squirm beneath him as the head

of his cock slips between my lips and pushes into my hot entrance.

A strangled cry pours from my mouth. My eyes squeeze shut tight.

"Shh," Alec hushes me, leaving gentle kisses on my jaw. "I'll go slow at first," he says in a comforting voice as he pushes in deeper, rocking his thick cock in and out of me, each time sliding in more. His girth stretches my walls with a sting that amplifies the pleasure still very much on the surface and pulsing through me.

In one swift move, Alec slams himself in me to the hilt and my head arches back, digging into the mattress as a silent scream leaves me. My walls tighten around him, spasming from the shock as he kisses my neck and grips onto my hips to keep me in place. He gives me a moment, but only a small one and my hands reach down to his, holding on with my nails digging into his skin.

"Alec," I murmur with the insecurity I feel. I don't know if I can take this. *It's too much.*

My head thrashes as he moves out slightly and then forces himself back in. He does it again and then once more, and I can already feel myself on the brink again. So close to being overwhelmed with another release.

Alec's hot breath travels down my skin like the lick of a flame as he groans, "Yes... Cum for me again. Let me feel you cum on my dick."

His dirty words are the last straw and for a second time, I come undone under him. But Alec doesn't wait for me. He doesn't let up. He continues to fuck me as the sensation washes through me and paralyzes me with unadulterated pleasure.

He pistons his hips, thrusting his thick length into me over and over again mercilessly. I scream out, "Alec!"

My heels dig into his ass, urging him on even though it's too much. Waves of intense heat roll through my body, burning every inch in slow creeping waves. Each one more threatening, more consuming than the last.

"Alec," I moan as I feel the impending fall of my release coming. I know it's close; I can feel it slowly making my fingers and toes curl. My head thrashes and I hold my breath, but Alec never stops.

He's ruthless and unforgiving as he continues to pound into me. The sound of me crying out his name and his low moans mix in the hot air. I struggle to breathe when he rides through my orgasm and forces more from me.

His hard body lies on top of mine, pinning me down and keeping me still while he pushes my release higher.

I almost cry out for him to stop, almost try to push him away. But the final wave of pleasure is too intense for me to do anything other than cry out and lie victim to its intensity.

Alec groans deep and low in the crook of my neck as his fingers dig harder into my hips with a bruising force as he erupts inside of me. I feel his thick cock pulse as hot streams leave him, filling me completely. He pumps his hips in short and shallow thrusts until we're both spent.

Leaving me on the highest high I've ever had, my body shaking and the cold air slipping between us as he rises between my trembling thighs.

I breathe heavily as my body lies limp on the bed, exhausted and sated and deliciously used. I'm vaguely aware that Alec's climbed off the bed, but the dipping and creaking of the mattress is a telltale sign. I listen to the faint patter of his bare feet as he slips into the en suite.

The warmth between my thighs leaks out slightly, and the realization wakes me enough to reach down and prevent it from slipping between my legs and onto the comforter. Before I have to shuffle awkwardly off the bed, Alec towers over me, pushing a hand against my chest. I fall easily for him and spread my legs.

He wipes my thighs and between my legs with a warm wet cloth, kissing the inside of my left knee and then pulling the blanket up over my naked body.

"No need for a dress shirt tonight," he whispers and kisses me quickly on the lips before disappearing again.

Although I smile and hum a small thanks of gratitude, inwardly I wish I'd just fallen asleep.

This situation is a nightmare because there's only one way for it to end.

With me shattered. I can already feel it happening.

Alec Kulls will ruin me.

Chapter 8

Lila

Tap, tap, tap. The only sounds in the room are of my fingers on the keys.

I should be in the cabin; I should be writing my article. I should be getting ready to leave more than anything.

Instead, I'm making myself comfortable in the library. *Alec's library.*

I lift my eyes as the door creaks open and Alec walks in, a bundle of small logs under his arm. My fingers stop moving for the first time in what must be hours.

"Why didn't you tell me it'd gone out?" he asks as he kneels in front of the fireplace. The smell of burnt wood drifts toward me as he picks up the cast iron poker.

"I thought you were busy," I tell him honestly. "That, and I'm..." I hesitate to say the truth, but I put the laptop down on the ottoman and shrug a bit as I confess, "I'm afraid of outstaying this welcome."

He huffs and doesn't answer me, putting in another log and stirring the hot embers, exposing bright oranges and reds.

"I don't mind," he says as he looks over his shoulder. He gives me a coy smile, letting his eyes drift over my body in a way that leaves no doubt he likes what he sees.

I pull my knees into my chest, and hide my face from him. I'm in his pajama pants and a white undershirt... also his.

We basically match, and I have no intention of getting out of these clothes.

At least I'm wearing clothes now. I passed out in Alec's arms and woke up to him hard and ready to fuck me again. And again. As I shift on the chair, I feel a dull ache between my thighs, and it only makes me want more of him.

I like to pretend that I'm trapped here in this massive estate with him, but I know I'm not. I have no excuse for practically shacking up with him over the course of this *business trip*.

This is bad. So, so bad.

But it feels *so good*. It's like the real world doesn't exist here. Everything is fresh and new, and Alec wants me.

I've never been with a man who's so honest. A man who doesn't mind catering to me, and acts like this is all completely natural. I can't help but think it's because it's temporary. Because I'm leaving.

The thought is unsettling and I shift in my seat, tearing my eyes from him.

"Hey," Alec gets my attention and makes his way over to me. He brushes his hands off on his pants but keeps his eyes on my face. "What's that look for?"

"What look?" I play dumb. I don't want to be the clingy hookup that got emotional before leaving. But that's exactly what I am.

This isn't me. I've never done a one-night stand before, simply because I don't know how to handle it. Let alone a few one-night-stands-on-vacation. If that's even a thing.

"Stop it, Lila." Alec admonishes me in a deep voice that sends shivers over my skin and hardens my nipples. "Don't overthink it."

He bends down, taking my chin between his thumb and forefinger and tilting my head up so I'm forced to look him in the eyes.

I pull away from him, hating that I'm getting emotional over whatever it is we have.

"It's easy for you to say," I tell him and instantly

regret it. He lets out a heavy sigh and takes a seat on the ottoman, pulling my legs into his lap.

"I hate that you think that," he says and I watch his expression for any indication he's lying, but he's not. Maybe this connection is real. But if that's true, it makes it all the harder to leave.

"Don't think about tomorrow," he says as he leans forward and braces his hands on the sofa on either side of my head. He towers over me, staring into my eyes. "We have right now, so let's hold on to right now."

I close my eyes as he leans forward, pressing his lips against mine for a sweet kiss. He deepens it and I react, moaning into his mouth and parting my lips for him. My hands reach up, gripping his shirt and pulling him closer to me.

I don't want this to end. I'm too afraid to say it out loud though. Too afraid to admit that I'm falling too soon, and too hard.

This was never supposed to happen.

Even as Alec moves his hand to my waist and pushes my legs apart with his hips, I know I can't stop myself.

I never had a chance with him.

Chapter 9

Lila

"I want a trinket," I say lightheartedly, although my heart is heavy. It's my last day here, and our time together is quickly coming to an end.

I spent most of yesterday in Alec's bed listening to the tales he remembers from when he was a child, or writing.

The words flow easily here. But I've only written poetry and short stories. Not anything related to the interview. That can wait till I get back home. I won't let it interrupt what this place is making me feel. The inspiration and muse are strong here. And I love it.

"A trinket?" Alec asks as he picks up a piece of pottery. It's handmade of clay with filigree work, painted deep green and coated with a gloss. It's beautiful and would be perfect for a candle holder. I take it from his hand, adding it to the small collection in the wicker basket that was at the front of the shop.

"*Trinkets*," I correct myself with a smile. This is the fourth shop we've been in, and every one is full of the most beautiful things. Handwoven blankets, old books with that aged smell I love, artisanal decor. And the food--I practically moan just thinking about it.

"Is the entire island like this?" I ask Alec as I raise a candle to my nose. I inhale the lavender scent deeply and close my eyes.

I love everything about this place. I can't help but think I'm being shortsighted, or maybe it's a case of the grass is greener on the other side. But I want to stay.

I don't want to go back to a small, cramped apartment where I don't know a soul and probably never will. I don't want to go back to an office that's constantly moving at a pace that's tiresome to keep up with.

I just want to go back to the cabin, or truthfully, home with Alec, and write.

I place the candle back down onto the shelf and frown as I shake off the uneasiness flowing through me. I don't know what's come over me, but this pining and longing for something I can't have needs to end.

I look up as Alec stiffens as the sight of someone

walking across the street catches his eyes. I follow his gaze and watch a small woman walk beside a man who looks so much like Alec. Maybe a bit older, since there are faint streaks of gray on his temples and he's not dressed in a suit, plus his hair is lighter. But they're definitely related. I sneak a glance at Alec, not letting him realize that I see, that I notice something is going on.

The woman seems so out of place. It's almost like she's scared, and I notice how the other people around them are watching, too. They have looks of sympathy on their faces.

"She's had a difficult pregnancy," the older woman behind the counter says in a soft voice. A voice meant for me alone, but Alec hears, too. He sucks in a breath and stares at the woman for a moment, but she meets his gaze evenly.

"Who are they?" I ask Alec.

He swallows before admitting, "My brother and his..." He doesn't finish, and I can tell why. There's something odd between them, something tense and uncertain. Something that scares them both. "Belle."

I take a look over my shoulder to see Alec's brother gentle a hand on the woman's waist. He pulls her closer to him and she lets him, seeming to melt into him. It's a gesture that makes my heart ache. There's a love there, but it's hurt and sad.

"Do you want to say hello?" I peek up at Alec after I ask him, but he simply shakes his head.

"Another time, perhaps," he says and turns his back to them, facing the woman and gesturing to the baubles in my arm.

"But I'm leaving," I protest without thinking. As if I have any say in who I meet from his family. I'm embarrassed for a moment, but only for the briefest of seconds, because he smiles down at me, brushing his fingers against my cheek.

"Why don't you stay?" Alec suggests. He lets out a heavy breath and shoves his hands into his suit pant pockets. "You could work from here, couldn't you?"

My heart flutters, loving that he wants me to stay. Maybe it's the romantic in me, the folklore, the beautiful surroundings, or maybe it's the way he looks at me.

I could. So easily.

I have to turn my head to hide my smile. It's foolish though. I clear my throat, shaking my head. "I can't stay," I tell him and even as I say the words, my heart hurts. This fling or whatever it is between us wasn't smart. How can I be so attached to someone so quickly? "I'm sorry," I tell him sincerely, the smile slipping and my true disappointment coming through. I feign another smile, expecting him to shrug it off, but he doesn't. His pale blue eyes stare deeply into mine, pinning me in place.

The air tenses between us, heating my blood and stealing my breath. It's not the reaction I imagined.

After a moment he nods once, and he doesn't play it off like he's unaffected. He takes a breath and then looks like he's going to say something, but instead he swallows thickly and looks away.

I'd love to stay here. The setting is an author's dream and the untold stories of Ketchikan are enough to tempt me, even if Alec wasn't into me like this. I truly want to stay here. I'm genuinely drawn to the land and the culture. There's a reason those who visit the island stay.

"I really can't," I whisper, both to myself and to Alec.

"One more night then?" he asks me in a low voice as he trails his finger over my shoulder, brushing my hair out of the way and planting a small kiss on my collarbone. I look up and into his eyes, so full of vulnerability and desire, a mixture of both that tempts me in the worst way.

I nod, not trusting myself to speak and close my eyes as he presses his lips against mine.

One more night, and then I have to leave.

He deepens the kiss, and it feels like so much more. Like he's giving me everything he has.

I'm almost afraid of staying with him. Afraid I'll never want to leave. But I know tomorrow I'll be gone. And I won't let fear keep me from having just one more night with him.

Chapter 10

Lila

The engine clicks and clacks and snarls. Like it's spitting, rather than rumbling. I stand on the deck, gripping the handle of my suitcase and watching the waves crash against the shore. They aren't harsh or threatening like they seemed to be the last time I was here. It's simply the way it is. It's never going to end; the waves will always batter away at the shore.

"I'm really sorry, Miss Travers," Drew says as he walks out of the cabin of the ship and to the very back of the boat, closest to where I'm standing on the wooden deck.

"What's wrong?" I ask him as the salty breeze whips my hair in front of my face. It's chilly today, colder than it has been and being near the ocean is only making it worse.

Drew's face crumples as he says, "It's going to be a few hours, maybe more before I fix her." He motions behind him with his thumb.

I glance to my right where three more boats are tied to the dock. "Surely there's another boat?" My heart beats faster as I think about having to stay here on this island, so close to Alec, for a while longer.

"It's been a while since they've been up and running and on this water," he says and runs his hand over the hair at the back of his head, looking over to the boats and then back to the cabin. "I'm sorry, Lila," he says with sympathy, climbing off the boat and onto the dock.

Fuck.

My thoughts immediately stray to Alec.

It doesn't matter that I want him. Or that he wants me, too.

That can't be enough, but as I question myself, I can't think of a damn thing else that matters.

Maybe it's fate, a little voice whispers in the back of my head, so full of hope.

"How long do you think?" I ask Drew as he takes off his gloves and taps them against his palm.

"No longer than a night I'd think," he answers and then waits for my response.

Just one more night. I tell myself it'll only be one

more night, but I already know I'm lying to myself. I was able to walk away once. I don't know if I'll be able to again.

I clear my throat and look over my shoulder, but before I can ask Drew, he answers the unasked question.

"You need a ride?"

Knock. Knock. Knock.

The bitter cold makes my knuckles hurt as I look between Drew, sitting in his car with the engine still purring in front of the Kulls' estate, and the closed door. My nerves are getting the best of me, and anxiety is racing through my blood.

"Don't turn me away," I whisper to the door and raise my fist again to knock harder, just as it swings open. Warmth flows from inside the house, and it makes the outdoors feel that much colder. My arm slowly falls to my side as Alec stands in the doorway, wearing nothing but a pair of slacks on that are hung low on his waist. His broad shoulders fill the span of the door as he takes a step closer to me.

"Alec," I speak his name just above a murmur. His pale blue eyes peer into mine, filled with questions and then the sound of Drew driving away takes his eyes from mine. It's only then that I feel I can breathe.

Shit, I think as I turn around and watch Drew pull away... with my suitcase in his car. He'll be back in a few hours either way, at least that's what he told me. But he could've waited, damn it. I swallow thickly, knowing I have nowhere to go. I'm stuck here and if Alec turns me away, I'll be all alone. I'll be leaving this beautiful place exactly how I came here. Alone.

"Lila, I thought you were leaving?" he asks and then a chill sweeps through me. Before I can answer he moves aside and pulls me into the house, wrapping his arm around my waist as if his hands belong on me.

He releases me long enough to shut the door, and I instantly miss his touch. I stare at his muscular back as he closes and locks the door, the click filling the silence. He turns slowly, spearing his fingers through his hair. "I thought you would have been gone already."

I clear my throat and answer. "I was supposed to," I confess. "But the boat is..." I falter over my words. "It's not working," I spit out.

"Oh," Alec's gaze falls to the floor for a moment, and his forehead creases. "So, you're only here for... how long?" His voice is filled with disappointment and it cuts me deep, making my heart pain.

"A few hours, maybe another day," I tell him. Why does it hurt so much to tell him that? It's only been days.

It shouldn't be this painful.

He nods his head and looks down the hall before forcing a smile to his face. "Well, let me feed you at least."

"I'm sorry, Alec," I whisper as he reaches for my coat and helps me slip it off.

He doesn't respond, merely hanging my coat up before turning back to face me. "Lila," he says and then licks his lips. "You know I don't want you to go."

I nod my head, my fingers intertwining with one another but they stop as he takes a step closer to me, filling the space between us. The heat from his body warms mine and draws me closer to him.

"I want you," he whispers, his lips trailing along the shell of my ear as he moves his body in front of mine, his fingers caressing down to the curve of my waist. And like a moth to a flame, my hands rest against his chest and I lean into his touch, wanting more of him.

He kisses my neck, an open-mouth kiss that makes my head lean to the right so I can expose more of myself to him.

"There's something real here," he says as he grips my ass and pulls me closer to him. The sudden movement makes me gasp.

"I don't think I can promise I'll take it slow, but I can promise to try," he says, staring into my eyes. The way he looks at me has me mesmerized. Trapped, even.

"If you just stay, I'll do whatever I can to keep you." He tells me words that make me want so much more. Words I've only dreamed a man like him would say to me.

I know it's not logical, and it's not safe on my part. Not for my career, or for my heart. It's reckless and naïve. But he's so right that there's something between us. *Something more.*

"I'm afraid," I tell him, and my words seem to float between us. They're riddled with the anxiety I feel. Knowing if I stay, it's all for him. I'd be committing so much to and trusting a man I barely know. But a man who makes me feel alive and cherished. A man I want more from. *More with.*

"I want you, Lila, and I'm afraid to let you go again," he says in a whisper. His weakness, his confession is what does me in.

I nod my head although there was never a question asked.

Nonetheless, it makes his expression change. "Stay with me?" he asks.

I nod again and say, "We can take it slow?"

He chuckles and breaks his gaze for a moment. "I'm not sure how slow, but I'll do my best." He lowers his forehead to mine and whispers, "I don't want to scare you off again."

"You didn't," I tell him honestly, gripping his arms and

looking deep into his eyes. "It wasn't you. It's just this..."

"It's intense," he says the words I'm thinking. It is. *It's overwhelming. It's too much.*

"It's perfect," he whispers against my lips and then gives me a quick kiss. He breaks it before I'm ready and I find myself nearly falling as he pulls away. A rough chuckle spills from his lips as I touch my fingers to my mouth.

"We're really doing this?" I ask him.

He takes my hand in his. "I want to," he answers. "I want you."

I could tell him so much more in this moment, but I'll save it for a later date. "I want you, too," I tell him.

He brings my hand to his lips and kisses my knuckles.

"We have plenty of time, Lila. Let's start with something to eat."

Chapter 11

ALEC

ONE WEEK LATER

The truth and perception are two different things.

"You know the town will talk," Drew says to my left as I look out over the ocean. We're deep in the forest on the very edge of the property. My grandfather used to take me here. He said this was the best position on the island, the most powerful. Because it's where the people come and go.

"They're already talking," he adds.

"I'm aware," I answer, not bothering to take my eyes away from the crashing waves. A heavy sigh leaves me, knowing my love is going to have questions and there's still a road ahead of us with twists and turns. But if they tell her anything that makes her question me, I'll simply answer her honestly. I finally look at him, shoving my hands in my pockets as I say, "She knows I'm head over heels for her, and soon she'll have a more important reason to stay." I turn on my heels without waiting for him and walk back to the family lodge.

Lila will be back soon.

The sticks break under Drew's weight as he hustles to catch up to me. "Are you sure it was wise?" he asks and I cock a brow at him, not knowing which part of this entire ordeal he's talking about.

"Was what wise?"

"The fake birth control?" he asks and I don't let my stride break. I don't let him see that I'm affected in the least. I don't know if the tradition had anything to do with what's between Lila and me, but I'm too chickenshit to go against it. And according to legend, the bond must be sealed with conception before the next full moon.

Losing Lila wasn't worth the risk. It's one of a few lies. I may have deceived her, but it's for us. She'll forgive me because what we have is real. It's so fucking obvious. I'll never let her go.

I shrug as we come up to the back porch of the lodge and I climb the three stairs, gripping the wooden railing to keep me grounded. I'm not sure how she'll react when she finds out I've lied.

But she knows the kind of man I am.

The kind who goes after what he wants. *Who* he wants.

That day I took the tincture I was so sure I'd prove to my brother how foolish he was being. It only took one article to prove how wrong I was. Lila's face stared back at me, and all I could do was read her articles. Everything she'd ever written, everything I could find online. I was infatuated the moment I saw her.

And I'll keep her with everything I have.

"I'm not sure she'll ever find that one out," I say, looking at him from the corner of my eyes and making sure the threat is clearly evident.

He raises his hands in surrender but says, "The pregnancy may give it away." His voice is low, careful to make sure no one can hear.

I stop just outside of the sliding glass doors. "I know it's not right to start it off like this," I start to tell him, thinking about every deal I planned and manipulated, every lie and deceitful action. It's not right, but this situation isn't normal.

"She'll forgive me if she ever finds out," I tell him with confidence. "My intentions are pure." I only want to love her. To keep her and have her. I'll spoil her with everything she could ever want or need. The lies were necessary. If she knew the truth, surely she would have run far and fast.

He nods at my admission, but his eyes flicker to the floor.

"What?" I ask him.

"So were your brother's," he answers me. My body tenses at the thought of Annabelle.

I clear my throat and ball my hands into fists as I say, "She's nothing like that." I take a step forward, closing the space between us as the anger builds. "*This is nothing like that.*"

I love my brother Marcus. I've always looked up to him, thought well of him. But what he's done, *what he's doing*, it's not right. I just don't understand why. There must be a reason.

Either way, my Lila is nothing like Belle and our situations aren't comparable.

"I'm not saying that," Drew answers me with strength in his voice although he cowers slightly. I calm my breathing, the adrenaline pumping hard in my blood.

"I'm not saying that at all," he repeats and takes a step back. "I'm just saying that maybe," he takes a breath and looks behind me, straightening his stance and looking casual. I peek over my shoulder to see Lila walking toward us. The pea coat she's wearing is a teal color that pops amongst the tree line, making her stand out even more.

The sight of her reddened cheeks and windblown

hair makes my body crave to touch her, to hold her. To keep her safe.

She's mine.

"I'm just saying," Drew says in a low voice, gaining my attention again. He swallows and lick his lips. "Be careful with her," he adds and his eyes search mine, a hint of worry evident.

I nod once and take a step backward. She's not his concern, but I'll put him at ease.

"If she wants to leave me," I start to answer him with the promise I know he needs, but I can't give it to him. "Then I'll convince her otherwise." I tell him the truth, and his gaze drops.

"I love her, Drew." My words make his eyes drift back up. I offer him something that I know will put him at ease, but unexpectedly, also puts me at ease. "I'll bring her to the shops often. She's curious and loves the town."

"Alec!" I hear her call out from behind me with happiness in her voice.

I quickly add, "If she ever looks anything but in love and happy in every way, tell me." I hold his gaze as I hear her call out again, the sounds of her coming closer to the porch getting louder and more evident.

As soon as I hear her boots hit the wooden deck, Drew nods his head. "I'll tell you," he says.

"And I'll listen," I reply and then quickly turn around

to face my love with a welcoming smile. My heart clenches thinking that one day, Drew may come to me and tell me she's unhappy. I won't let it happen.

A gorgeous smile widens across her face as she comes closer, and I walk to meet her halfway. "Good morning," I tell her and then press my lips against hers, wrapping my arms around her waist and pulling her into me, muffling her greeting. She moans softly as her lips mold to mine and I only break the kiss because I know Drew's behind us.

The blush creeps up to her cheeks as she bites her bottom lip and tucks her hair behind her ear shyly.

It only makes me want her more.

"Hi Drew," Lila says sweetly although it only makes her cheeks redder, and she can't look him in the eyes. She's so innocent and pure, so easy for me to take for myself.

A soft wind blows and I tuck a loose strand of hair back behind her ear and kiss her one last time before moving to the doors.

"Let's go in," I tell her and then glance at Drew. His expression is one of contentment at least as he nods and says hello in return. "This house is filled with stories."

And I'll tell her every one of them.

One day she'll understand.

Until then, I know she has feelings for me. And what I feel for her is real.

Everything else be damned.

A Note from the Author:

I am determined to, one day, return to this world. I have a feeling that day will come sooner rather than later, and when it does, Lila and Alec will have more to their story and each of the Kull brothers will have their own stories as well.

Until then, I hope you enjoyed *Infatuation*.

Desires In The Night

Chapter 1

Valarie

The rain has stopped and the absence of the battering against the car roof makes the hushed sounds of the radio I'd turned down sound louder. My tired eyes flicker to the radio station on the dash; I don't recognize it and a few scans through the next dozen stations prove to find me nothing of interest. With a flick of my wrist it's silenced and only the hum of the car engine and the warm night air ride with me.

The lights go bye quickly, illuminating and then darkening the old country roads. They're asphalt, but the back ways of getting around. The mountains on the right side of the road are covered in thick trees that hide the light of the moon. But the stars on the left side are bright and give enough of a soft glow that it's comfortably dark.

The gentle light and sweet smells of late spring make me feel as if maybe this was the right decision. Maybe it is the right choice.

I'm close. I know I am.

A soft sigh leaves me as I loosen my grip on the wheel and try to readjust in my seat.

I'm so close to my destination. How long I'll stay; I'm not sure. But every second I get closer, is another second the anxiety stirs into desire in the pit of my stomach.

I read the large green signs as I drive by. Looking for a name that's familiar. A few of them resonate in me. Sending a chill down my spine and a heated desire straight to my core. *I'm so close.*

The back roads may not be familiar to me. But they hold memories. Memories I've dreamed about in the last few months and images that have haunted me.

They play in my mind as I drive down the windy roads.

There's no one here, not a soul out this late at night.

I remember how he pushed me down into the dirt. How my knees scratched on the pavement. I can still remember the sound of the officer's zipper being pulled down and the tug of my hair at the base of my head.

He tasted sweet. I only wanted to lick him at first.

Just to tease him like he was doing to me that night.

Just the drop of precum that sat in the slit of his dick. It glistened in the evening light with the silence surrounding us only interrupted by my heavy breathing.

My thighs clench as I remember him punishing me. Shoving himself deep down the back of my throat. As far as he could until I gagged.

But I was eager for more. I didn't care if it was too much for me to take.

My knees were dirty, my hands trembled as my parked car hid us from view.

It was quick and over before I was ready.

That was the first time, years ago when I was only in my early twenties. Young and stupid. Wanting a thrill and more than that, wanting to be fucked the way I'd always dreamed of. There are some desires that are best for the night.

According to the GPS, I'm now driving on that very road. Searching out the same desire as if I might stumble upon it before I get to a place I've never wanted to be.

The last time I was here, I couldn't wait to leave. A small Podunk town wasn't the place where my dreams would be made... or so I thought.

My gaze flickers to the clock on the GPS. Estimated time of arrival is only seventeen minutes. It's odd how my heart sinks and a sense of loss flows through me as I turn onto the main road.

But the loss is quickly forgotten on the deserted road.

Only because it's not quite deserted.

My fingers just barely tip the turn signal down, my grip tightening on the wheel as I spot him.

The parked cop car immediately follows behind me.

My heart beats harder and I can't stop myself from staring into the rear view mirror, searching for his face.

For his hard jaw, just barely speckled in rough stubble. His short hair, buzzed on the sides and longer on top. And his eyes. The way his dark green eyes pierced through me, shredding me of anything that could save me.

And the second I see it's him, I lose myself in the memories and desires that have been devouring my every waking moment.

I'll remember the power and hunger in his eyes that first night on the side of the road forever.

Thud, thud, thud, my heart hammers as the seconds pass.

The tension cuts off my breathing and I can't stand it.

My nerves get the best of me before he can even turn his lights on, forcing me to pull over on the right, right next to a patch of tall oak trees.

Or maybe it's not nerves, it's desperation. It must be, because I can't breathe until he's pulled right behind me and parked.

Closing my eyes, I try to swallow, I try to steady my breathing.

My imagination runs wild for only a moment. Hearing my small feet crash through the fallen branches and leaves on the bed of the small forest, as I run from him. How he'd topple over me, catching up to me quickly.

My lips kick up into a smirk as I turn my keys and click the ignition off. He'd only let me get as far as he wanted.

And then he'd take me. In the dark of the night.

My eyes raise at that thought and to the sound of his police car door shutting behind me. Only a deserted street lies ahead. No one to see what I truly want.

He didn't even have to turn his lights on, let alone the siren.

I stare at his broad shoulders as he stalks towards me. The dark blue uniform is stretched taught over his muscular chest. There's something about that dip just beneath his throat too. The lights from his car shine behind him and cast shadows over his high cheek bones.

I close my eyes listening to the sound of his boots approaching.

I know exactly what I'm going to do. And what I'm going to let him do to me.

But this is my guilty pleasure. It's everything I've been dreaming about for months.

Chapter 2

Alex

My dick is already hard. I've been waiting far too long for her to come back.

She doesn't know that I knew she was coming tonight.

Maybe she thought she could sneak into town without telling me. Maybe she thought she'd make it all the way to the Inn without having run into me.

She should know better than that.

A deep rough groan is stifled in the back of my throat as my dick strains against the zipper of my slacks. I've been waiting for an hour in that exact spot. This is the perfect location. No one comes out to this part of town this late at night. She knows that too. She had to know.

My heart flickers as I get closer and see her head resting back, her eyes closed. Her chest rises slowly in the thin cotton shirt. Her skin is flushed, the pale blush rising up to her cheeks.

My boots scuffle the small broken pieces of asphalt beneath my feet and her long lashes flutter as she turns her head to face me.

A moment passes as I take her in. From the stray locks of dark brown hair to the small freckles on her cheeks that trickle down to her shoulder. Even with the faint light and tired eyes from driving for hours, she's fucking gorgeous.

"Officer?" her sweet voice is shaky. Her entire body is trembling just slightly. Even as she grips the seatbelt laying across her lap. I know her name without needing her license.

But she called me "Officer" and if she wants to go back to playing like we used to, who am I to say no?

"License and registration." Every slight movement makes the tension hotter. Her soft locks of hair fall down her back as she reaches over to the glove compartment. She lets her ass stick out and takes a second too long after she's found what she's looking for and a satisfied groan leaves me.

I don't have the patience to wait any longer. But for

her and her forbidden fantasies... fuck, I'd do anything to have her.

The darkness in her doe eyes swirls with recognition as I lean forward, setting my forearm onto the roof and lowering my face to the window.

"I'm going to need more than this Miss."

"Mrs." She's quick to correct me, her previously soft and sultry voice ringing out clear in the night air. My eyes search hers for a long time. Besides her ragged breathing and my heart pounding in my chest, all I can hear are the sharp chirps of the crickets in the thicket of the forest to our right.

"Mrs. then. I'm going to need a little more from you," I tell her.

"What would you like?" she asks as her eyes flicker from mine to the lock on the door. She bites down on her lower lip and rings the seatbelt in her hands.

My words escape me for a moment. Only a moment as I remember crashing my lips against hers and biting down on that lip myself. So sweet and innocent. The night I met her, that's all I thought she was. I don't like to admit it, but sometimes I can be wrong.

"You're going to need to get out of the vehicle," I tell her as I slip my hand in through her window and pull the handle myself.

I can't help how my lip twitches into a smile at her

faint gasp.

With her eyes cast down and her lips parted, Valarie slowly slips from the car and I nearly groan out loud from the sight of her. Her pale yellow skirt sways around her thighs and her heels click on the pavement.

The car door clicks shut softly as I watch her chest raise and fall with each heavy breath she's taking. So innocent. She did this on purpose to tempt me. This woman standing in front of me isn't at all the sweet little thing she appears to be.

"Follow me," I give her the command as she clasps her hands, so eager to touch me. I know exactly what she needs, what dirty thoughts are playing through her head.

The second I splay my hand on her lower back, it's like a bolt of electricity that shoots through me. My body recognizing hers, *needing* hers.

My pace quickens as I practically push her to my car. Her thigh bumps into the hood and makes her gasp, but grabbing her wrist, I pull her around to the side opposite the street so we're out of view. She stumbles and nearly falls, making her wavy hair cascade in front of her face.

"Officer, what's the meaning of this!" she protests and I'd laugh if I didn't feel like I needed her lips wrapped around my cock, more than I needed the air I breathe.

"I don't have time for games, Mrs..." I don't finish the thought as I unbuckle my belt, "on your knees."

"Officer," she breathes in protest even as she licks her lips and falls onto her knees on the hard ground instantly. Again she holds her hands, ringing her fingers around one another as I take my time, unbuckle my belt and the slowly sliding the zipper down.

The sight of her like this is everything I've wanted since the last time we did this.

"I know you know what to do," I tell her under my breath as the dark night seems that much darker. My fingers spear in her hair and I make a fist, bringing her forward, but my dirty little slut is already sucking me down. Her fingernails digging into my thighs with eagerness for more. Shielding her teeth with her lips she takes in as much of my dick as she can, into her hot greedy mouth.

My head falls back with nothing but pleasure as the intense sensation sings in my blood. The need to fuck her mouth like it's her cunt rides me hard, but I hold back just slightly. Just enough to let her have some fun.

Her cheeks hollow and she tries to swallow my dick. The sensation feels too fucking good. My toes curl as I grunt and shove myself deeper down her throat. Again and again until I have to stop. I pull away, making my dick pop out of her mouth before she can make me cum.

"I want you," she barely gets the words out as she tries to catch her breath.

She wipes her mouth with the back of her hand. Still on her knees, she stares up at me like I can command her. And so I do.

"Beg for it," I tell her knowing all the things she's told me she wants.

Shame heats her cheeks, making them flushed and that much more gorgeous.

"Show me how much you've missed me."

Chapter 3

Valarie

"You want this so bad don't you?" He asks me as if he doesn't know how much I've wanted to relive this night. "You're dying for it. Your cunt needs me."

"Please, fuck me." I have no shame this time. I want him. I'm throbbing against him with desire and I have no intention of being denied. I place my splayed hand against his chest and push against him. With little resistance, he leans back against his car, slowly dropping to the ground until he's seated on the dirt with me, his hooded eyes finding mine.

I lean into him and place my lips at his ear. "I want you. And you better not fucking deny me."

"Fuck me then," he groans and takes my head in his hands. His lips crash hard against mine. His strong tongue runs along the seam of my lips and I part for him. My pussy heats with anticipation as he nips at my bottom lip, making me moan. I can feel him stroking himself and that knowledge makes my skin heat even more. I need him inside of me. Filling me and stretching me with his cock.

I position myself so that the head of his dick is at my entrance. I'm already needy, and wet and I didn't even bother wearing panties. I'm that desperate. He stares into my eyes with his lips parted as I gently glide down his massive cock.

"Oh my God," I moan at the heavenly feel; it's so fucking good. I can barely breathe as his cock sinks into me. Fuck!

There's a hint of pain and I'm sore instantly. It's been way too long. I can feel my face scrunch as his fingertips dig into my hips and he shoves himself roughly inside of me. Although it hurts for a moment, the fullness makes my body sing with pleasure.

Even with the intensity of what we're doing, the second my eyes meet his, none of it matters. His heated gaze stops me, every part of me. He holds me in a trance of relentless need and desire. It's all I can see, all I can feel and I can't move until he grips my waist and let's out a deep groan of need. Even still, his gaze doesn't leave mine.

I move a few inches up and down and then sink all the way down his length, whimpering as the mixed sensation of pleasure and pain causes my limbs to tremble. I still as his dick hits my wall, pushing against it, and let my tight pussy relax around him. My head falls onto his shoulder as the hot sensation overwhelms me. I can barely move, barely do anything at all.

He takes my head in his hand and kisses me sweetly. His lips are soft and I quickly deepen it. Wanting more of him and of this. I want this night to be burned into my memory just as that night was years ago. He pulls back first, breathing heavily and staring back at me with wild eyes.

"I thought you wanted to fuck?" he says in a calm and rough tone that doesn't match any of this. All it does is make me simper, the desire and need to fuck what's mine comes back to me full force.

I lick against his lips and he gives me his tongue to suck. I moan into his mouth as I pick my body up and then glide down his length, my arousal makes the movement effortless, although his girth is still stretching me. I lean back and pick up my speed while my hands rest on his muscular pecks. Riding him at my own pace. The chill in the air sends goosebumps down my flesh. Hardening my nipples and heightening the sensation that much more.

His hands stay at my hips, but he doesn't control the movements. His head leans forward and he takes my nipple into his mouth, through the thin fabric of my blouse and sheer bra; he bites down and pulls back. Fuck yes! The simple movement makes my pussy ache. I arch my back at the spike of pleasure and wanton heat in my core. But just as soon as he gives me the delicate mix of pleasure and pain, he takes it away.

He relaxes against the car watching my pussy move over his dick with a hungered look in his green eyes. His heated gaze of adoration sends yet another surge of arousal through me.

"I want you so fucking bad," I whimper, my words laced with the loneliness I've felt for too long.

"I'm right here," he tells me and his words draw my eyes to his lips, and then to his throat as I watch him swallow thickly. He's mine. I have him again.

He rocks his hips in a sharp motion and it forces me to cry out as he tears through me quickly. Fuck!

My clit hits against his pelvis every downward stroke and the moisture that's gathered there makes my pleasure all the more intense.

I stop my movements and stare at him. He's letting me ride him. He's given me control. But it's false control. I find myself wanting him to fight for it. I want him to *take* me. It takes a moment for him to look up at me. He bucks his hips against me, causing me to moan as his eyes find mine. As we both catch our breath he asks, "What's wrong?"

I pause for a moment before admitting the truth, "I want you to fight me."

Before I can blink, he's spun us around in the dirt, forcing us both to our feet as he stands and then crushed my body against the car with his.

I can barely breathe as my back presses against the cold window of the car and I stand on shaky legs. His forearm presses against my shoulders and pushing against him proves useless. He's a hard wall of brick and he has me right where he wants me. I can't move or fight him in the least.

His lips crash hard against mine, stealing what little air I have in my lungs before he spins my body around, pinning me against the car. My legs are on either side of his with his hard dick nestled between the slick folds of my pussy. Both my wrists are captured in one of his hands and held above my head. My breasts are pressed against the car with his heavy chest pushing against my back. I gasp in shock. *Holy fuck!* My heart races in my chest. His speed and strength are terrifying and invigorating at the same time. It wasn't like this before. But then again, we're both in need and the time for playing is over.

His other hand slips between the car and my body, and he circles my clit with heavy, unrelenting pressure. "Oh, my God," I moan against the window. The feeling is so intense I try to move away, but I'm trapped. I can hardly move any part of my body.

He whispers into my ear, "you questioning my dominance, sweetheart?" My pussy clenches at his words, feeling empty without him inside me. I shake my head slightly the best I can.

He slams his dick inside of me to the hilt and I scream out his name while my orgasm rips through my body. He groans into my neck. "You feel so fucking good."

His words bring me that much closer to yet another release as he starts rutting me from behind. Each thrust harder and faster than the last.

I love every bit of what he's doing to me. I can hardly take it, but at the same time I want more. I want all of him. I need all of him. My heart clenches in agony. I find myself wanting to beg, but I don't know what for. His lips kiss over the skin of my shoulder and neck hungrily.

He nips my ear and sucks on my neck, quickening his pace.

The sound of his hips slamming into me fuels my need to cum. I try to push against the car, to move away as the feeling becomes too much. The metal is so cold against my skin. Everything is so cold except for him. I need to be closer to him but the sensation is too much. I can't. I can't.

I try everything to escape, but I'm pinned. I can't get away from the intensity of need running through my body, heating and numbing every inch of me.

"No no, sweetheart. You wanted me to fuck you like this, remember?" The danger in his voice is intoxicating. I was a fool to think I could fight him. But I love it so much. The taste of forbidden and the excitement of what he can do to me. Fuck, I've missed it. I've missed him.

"Take it sweetheart." His growl makes my pussy clamp down and just as I'm about to cum all over his dick again, he roughly pinches my clit making me scream his name. My strangled moan carries through the empty night as my lungs stop and my entire body tenses. The heat travels through me in waves. Hard and fast and crashing through my shaking body.

I've never cum so hard in my life. I pulse on his dick as my body trembles uncontrollably. I feel him release at the same time. His dick throbs inside of me, heightening my own pleasure.

Even with the fog of desire clouding every thought, I smile against the car, sagging my body and feeling the cold against my bare skin. This was everything I've needed.

He's what I need. A truer statement doesn't exist.

"Fuck." He breathes into my neck. "I've missed you so fucking much." He breathes heavily and his words come out with desperation. "I'm not letting you go again."

As the high from what we've done starts to fade into the dark night, my ragged breath comes back to me.

And as it does, a pair of lights shines down the road signifying a car driving towards us.

"Shit, shit, shit."

Chapter 4

Alex

"F uck," I mutter beneath my breath, still stumbling with my belt as I hear the car roll up. Dammit Jimmy. He was a cock block in high school and I suppose some things never change.

I round my car and head towards the parked cop car as the passenger window rolls down.

"Everything OK here, Alex?"

I can hear Valerie's heavy breathing as I walk out onto the asphalt.

"Yeah Jimmy everything is fine." I turned around looking over my shoulder to see Valerie. Her skin is still flush from what we've just done but she's smoothing out her skirt as she steps to the side of the car and comes into view.

"Actually I have somebody I'd like you to meet," I tell him with a proud smile on my face as I wrap my arm around her shoulder. Valerie's soft body molds to mine and her arm squeezes around my hip. "Jimmy, this is my wife, Valerie. I've been dying for you to meet her."

"Well I'll be," Jimmy says leaning across the dashboard and sticking his hand out the window for Valerie take it.

When we met all those years ago, she scooped me up within weeks and took me back to her hometown. I've always wanted to be a police officer and it just made sense to leave with her.

She met me as a kid playing pretend. It was just a Halloween party and just a costume of the man I wanted to be. A night of flirting turned into so much more when I followed her home. Halloween is for pretend and recklessness. And so I thought my sweet angel would only be with me for a night. But Valerie's proved me wrong since the day I met her.

"All Alex has been doing since he's been here, is talk about you." Jimmy's comment gets a chuckle from Valerie.

Her sweet smile and soft voice is everything to me. I've missed her so damn much since I've come back here. "We can't thank you enough for sending him down here during this hard time."

Valerie takes a step towards Jimmy's car, both of her hands resting on the open window as she answers him with sincerity. "I'm so sorry to hear about the fire."

"It's mostly all fixed up now," Jimmy says confidently, although his gaze shifts behind us and into the dark forest. He's an emotional man and the loss has been hardest on him. "But I can't tell you how wonderful it's been to have Alex back here."

"He's always talked about coming back," Valerie says, looking over her shoulder. Her hair falls down to her lower back.

My grip on her tightens as I say the words, "it's always been home to me." Valerie's eyes go and soften as she nods just slightly. Just for me.

When I left years ago, I was young and in love. And I'd still do anything for her. She knows this place calls to me though.

As I look at her and then back at Jimmy, he seems to understand exactly what we've been doing here. I can practically see the light bulb turn on in his head. He swallows thickly and all the warm welcome and good wishes seem to leave him.

The leather of his seat groans as he leans back in his seat and gives us a wave. "I'll be seeing you two tomorrow night at the barbecue?" he asks and we answer in unison, "we'll be there."

"I'm really looking forward to meeting everybody," Valerie says. There's an eagerness in her voice but also hesitation. I know she never wanted to stay here and I'd never keep her here if she didn't want to stay.

I can't help that this place will always be home to me though and will always be the place where we first met. Where I first fell in love.

"Well, all right; till tomorrow night then," Jimmy says and drives off before Valerie can get another word out. She's left with her hand still in the air as the red of his rear lights become smaller in the distance.

I wrap my arm tight around her waist and pull her closer to me, even though her eyes are watching the cop car.

"Come here," I pull her in close and up against me, her small breasts press against my chest. Her warmth makes the hot summer night feel cold around us. I can't get enough of her. The tip of my nose brushes her before I lean down for a long slow kiss. The kind that I've missed every day since I've been here.

It's been months since the fire broke out. It cost our town some of my childhood heroes. My best friend's fathers and mothers. There's nothing like a tragedy to bring family back together. I left as soon as I could, transferring out here, but my heart stay behind until she could come with me. And now that summers out and schools over. She only has a few months to be with me. Unless she's thought about what I asked. A wish. I can only hope she knows how much it means to me.

"I missed you so much," she tells me, as she leans against me, her fingers gripping onto me like I'll float away if she lets me go. Her cheek presses against my chest and I breathe her in.

I've missed you too," I tell her as my heart twists with the pain of being away from her for so long.

"I don't want to leave you again for so long," she whispers, letting her words linger in the hot night air.

"Stay with me then." I tell her and my heart pings. It's been easy for me, but she'll be giving up her job and starting over. I know there are positions available here, but I don't know if she's ready to move.

Her voice cracks and she has to swallow before looking me right in the eyes, "I can do that," she tells me and I can feel how much she means it. "I'm here to stay."

"You mean it?" I ask her although I don't know why. I can hear it in her voice.

"Always, Alex. I love you."

I crush my lips to hers, pulling her closer and then letting my hands roam down her curves. I've missed her more than a man should miss his wife. It takes everything in me to break the kiss, knowing we have to drive in separate cars before we get to the Inn, my family's place. But we'll be there soon and then I'll have her all to myself.

"I love you too." I whisper against her lips, slowly prying myself away from her. "Always."

Keeping Secrets

Fair warning before you start reading. I write gritty stories with twists that hold a darker edge. This short story turned into something I wasn't expecting and may be different from what you're expecting as well. Either way, I hope you enjoy it and love their tale like I do.

Chapter 1

Ella

It's all white. Everything in the bridal suite is white.

I suppose that's the way weddings should be. Not that I would know. It's not my wedding.

The sound of zippers being zipped up and hairspray being sprayed mixes with the chatter spilling from smiling, red lips.

"The red is perfect," Sara says, but the bride doesn't hear. "It matches everything." *That* catches the bride's attention.

"Nothing is done." Her eyes are wide and nearly spilling tears. "There's not a thing set up upstairs."

The bridal suite is on the first floor and the wedding will be on the second floor of this reclaimed farmhouse.

I down the champagne still in my flute that I've been sipping to calm my nerves. Aiden's going to be here, standing only a few feet from me. With pictures being taken every minute, videographers and photographers too, there's no way I'll be able to deny what I feel for him when the pictures are printed. Aiden's always said he can read the truth in my eyes.

What's the saying? Wearing your emotions on your sleeve? I absolutely do that, and even if this dress doesn't have sleeves, my emotions will be there, ready to show every one of the guests at the wedding exactly how I feel for a long-lost ex. They know he was my everything and they think him going to war is what broke us apart.

But they don't know the truth.

"I'm sure they're getting everything set up. There are still five hours before the guests come, and they can set everything in half that amount of time," I quickly say to Viv, the bride, and my best friend. Her pale blue eyes whip to mine, pleading with me to tell her that's the absolute truth.

"Seriously, it doesn't take long and everything will be perfect."

"I don't think the cake is here yet," one of the other bridesmaids says as she walks into the suite. The phone in her hand has her attention as the door clicks shut and everyone stays silent, waiting for the bride to go off at one more setback, that's not at all a setback.

"I need to call her, right now." Viv storms off and away from me, her silk white robe clutched at her chest. So, I settle back in the corner, nestle in my chair, and pretend not to think of Aiden, the counterpart to me, and a groomsman in the wedding.

He came back a different man, but the man I love was still there. I've been desperate for the love we once had, but we can't show love for one another with our kinds of secrets.

"Hey." I hear Lauren before I see her, and then hear the champagne as she pours it into my empty flute. "You okay?"

Her makeup is flawless, a perfectly plucked brow raised as she waits for me to answer her, pulling a chair closer to me.

I have to clear my throat and take a sip of the sweet bubbly before I can look her in the eye.

"Just nerves," I answer her with a faint shrug and forced smile. "I swear I'm more nervous than Viv is," I joke.

Lauren's gaze wanders across my face, judging me for honesty, and I'm sure I fail her test. Her words are softly spoken, "You haven't been the same since the party last week."

A thump and a flutter compete in my heart and my throat closes as she asks, "Is it because of Aiden? I know you guys have been together on and off, right?"

She's pushing for answers; answers I won't give. I'm not ready to, not today of all days.

I won't do or say anything at all to make a scene at Viv's wedding. I would feel fucking awful if I did. She and Jason have been together since high school and this day is far overdue.

Lauren's right, though. I haven't been the same since the party. The joint bachelor and bachelorette party.

That night changed everything. I knew it would never be the same when I walked into the crowded room, but I only felt the presence of one man. Aiden's eyes were on me before I'd even slipped my pea coat off. As the thin wool slipped down my bare shoulders, I watched his gaze turn into that of a predator, sizing me up as his prey.

The music was loud, the laughter louder, but I swear I could hear how his breathing hitched. His crisp dress shirt pulled tighter across his broad shoulders and with his shirt sleeves rolled up, I could see how the muscles in his forearms tightened as he gripped the armrest when I walked past him to go to Lauren and Viv, in the far corner of the room.

They were focused on their martinis. I was focused on how Aiden's gray eyes pierced through me and how his tight grip turned his knuckles white.

I have to remind myself where I am and who I'm with

before I let my thoughts get away from me. Slipping my hand to the dip in my throat and then lower, I let my fingers trace what's hanging on the end of my necklace, tucked just beneath the thin silk of the robe.

"I'm fine," I tell her shaking out my hands and plastering a wide smile onto my face. "Her being tense and anxious is just working me up."

"Okay, keep your secrets. I have a bet with Amy that you're fucking him, just so you know."

"She thinks you two fucked that night," Lauren's gaze stays glued to my face, waiting for a confirmation.

Although my heart races, I play along with Lauren's goading.

No one knows what happened the night of the party. And I don't know if I can keep this secret, one of many, for that long. Not when I know I'm going to see him.

"You two make the stupidest bets," I tell her with an evil grin and then lean in to confess to her in a hushed whisper, "And don't you know I'm a virgin?"

She outright laughs at my joke, even though it makes my heart pound harder.

"Nothing, absolutely nothing, is ready," Viv shrieks with a cracked voice before dropping her phone to the ground and falling onto the sofa across the bridal suite.

I take that as my cue, grateful for the distraction. Standing up abruptly, I'm quick to talk over everyone else, trying to comfort her.

"I'll go find the event coordinator right now." I can feel Lauren's eyes on me, but I ignore her and wrap the tie of my robe tighter so I can leave the room and feel somewhat decently covered. We all have matching scarlet robes, other than the bride's white one of course.

"What's her name again?" I ask.

"Sheryl," Viv's voice is weak but hopeful. She's not a bridezilla per say, but she's certainly emotional today.

"I'm sure everything is fine," I tell her and give her a small smile as I head to the door, "But I'll get a timeline and a checklist." With a firm nod, I exit and nearly collapse against the door. With my own emotions running wild, I lean against the hardwood and breathe for a moment, the faint chatter of voices muffled behind me, and the clanging of folding tables being set up echoing through the wooden ceiling above me.

Aiden is somewhere close. Somewhere smoking cigars and laughing with Jason, joking about how he's ending his bachelor days. I can do this I remind myself. I have to. After tonight, things will be different. No more hiding, no more secrets.

I don't know how they can't read it on my face.

I've kept secrets before, but not like this. But we all do foolish things for the ones we love.

Chapter 2

Aiden

I'd recognize her voice in a crowd anywhere, at any time. Even the soft hum that spills from her lips when she's listening to a good story.

"And the centerpieces will be placed like this. She wants the larger candle on the inside," I hear Ella say calmly as I stand at the bottom of the stairwell. The florist gives me a simple smile as she continues to pin ivory tulle up along the railing. It looks like she's just gotten started.

I know the bridal suite is in the back, but I take the stairs one at a time, following the sweet voice as her words drift down the stairwell.

"I've got it all and it's all under control. Please tell her not to worry." A tall woman in a silver tweed suit with her hair up in a tight bun stands beside Ella as I peek around the corner, "It's all under control," she repeats.

My eyes drift to the short silk robe, and then lower to the tanned legs on full display.

"I told her that already, but now that I've talked to you, I'm sure she'll feel better," Ella smiles, her long brunette hair already pinned up and braided. Just seeing that gorgeous smile and the flush of her cheeks tugs at the corner of my lips. My gaze drifts down her chest to her slender fingers, and my cock hardens instantly.

I lose control around Ella, I always have. She has a way of bringing out a side of me that's possessive and unpredictable.

I'd do anything to have her and keep her. But what she does to me... I groan low and deep in my chest as I watch the staff leave her all alone in the expansive room upstairs. There's not a soul in sight but her.

My jaw clenches, remembering how I lost control at the party, in the back laundry room.

Everything in the last two years disappeared into nothing and all I knew was that I needed her to be mine again.

I wanted everyone to know it. I wanted them to hear her scream my name. Instead, she clawed down my back and sank her teeth into my neck, leaving a bruised mark as I fucked her ruthlessly.

Precum leaks from me while remembering how good it felt to have her against the wall, pounding into her tight cunt while everyone we knew was just beyond a thin wall.

Before I can turn the corner, two men carrying a large white box enter, their simple black shirts have a cake on the front of them. And on cue, Ella claps her hands in delight, elated that the wedding cake has arrived.

"I'll go tell the bride," she tells them with a pep in her step that I haven't seen in so long. A darkness has clouded my judgment for years. I didn't know enlisting in the Army would change everything. Not just how I felt about Ella, but how I feel about myself and everything I've done.

I never questioned whether or not I would love her still. I always knew I would. There's nothing that could have taken me from her, or so I thought.

Ella disappears down a small hall, heading down the back stairwell, and so I turn around, going back the way I came.

Running a hand down the stubble of my jaw, I take the path that leads me to her. Taking my time so she'll be there before I am. *Although, I didn't come for her*, I have to remind myself.

My knuckles rapped against the door to the suite, knock knock knock.

"Who is it?" a few voices call out at once and someone

tells me, "If it's the groom tell him to fuck off. He can't see her yet!"

A genuine smile is stamped on my face when the door opens two inches. "I'm serious," Lauren says, and I respond, "It's just me. Should I fuck off too?"

She cocks a brow and takes a peek behind her. I know she's looking to find Ella and the smile slips. Soon they'll look at us differently. They'll never understand, but they won't deny what she is to me.

Soon everything will go back to the way it was supposed to be.

"Her husband-to-be isn't anywhere near." I pick up the small black, velvet box from my pocket and hold it in front of me, "I just have a gift."

Vivian pushes Lauren out of the way, pulling the door open wider and staring up at me with wide eyes, "From Jason?" she asks breathlessly.

My brow cocks as I say, "Maybe 'gift' was the wrong word." I clear my throat and give her a tight smile as the excitement drains from her expression. "I was told the ring was needed. For the ring bearer?" Jason needed someone to deliver it, and I was more than happy to oblige.

I'm not sure Vivian ever liked me, even though Jason was my best friend for as long as I can remember. She took him away when we were in high school, but she gave me something in return during our first year of college.

Ella. Her friend she thought would hit it off with me. She had no idea how right she would be. Sweet and quiet, but full of vulnerability, Ella was perfect for me. It only took a single date, a single kiss to know it. Even if she did make me wait for months to have her.

Still, she was perfect and I knew one day she'd be my wife.

The thought splinters the barely-healed crack in my heart. The pain of losing her never leaves.

Vivian turns her back to me, searching in a large cardboard box for something, not bothering to tell me to come in, so I stand where I am, waiting.

When I broke up with Ella, knowing it was what I needed to do when I came back from the war, Viv didn't hide her hate for me. And I get it. She found out who I was related to on the same day. Ella told her everything, so she knew the moment that Ella knew. A sad smile tugs at my lips. Viv didn't know everything of course. How could she? She wasn't Ella; she couldn't read the truth between the lines like Ella could.

I wish I could take it back. I wish I could change it all.

It took years of therapy to learn you can never go back. You can only take advantage of the day you're living. Tomorrow is never promised.

"I'll take that," the bride's sister-in-law tells me, slipping closer to me and yanking the box from my hand. It's her son that'll be walking down the aisle. "I've already got the box," she tells me.

I can feel Ella's gaze on me, begging me to look at her, to speak to her, to give her more than I am now.

Scratching the back of my head and attempting to make Viv a friend again, I tell her, "You look beautiful, Viv. The blushing bride suits you well."

As if she truly wanted to play the part, she blushes shyly. "He's going to go crazy when he sees you," I add.

"We have a bet going that he's going to cry," Lauren says, leaning against the back wall and grinning.

"Do you really think so?" she asks genuinely and I nod.

"He's lucky to have you, Viv," I tell her and mean it. What they have is love. I know exactly what it feels like and what it looks like. When you can't go to sleep because you only want to sleep next to one person who's miles away. When you hear their voice and everything else goes quiet so you can focus on the cadence of their voice and try to remember the sound for as long as you can. Jason didn't join the Army; he didn't go through a long-distance relationship like Ella and I did. But he looks at Viv the same way I used to look at Ella.

The way I'm trying not to now.

My gaze scans the room and I tell them all, "You all look stunning." My eyes land on her, on Ella, as I watch as those sweet lips part and add, "Gorgeous."

Chapter 3

Ella

The camera flashes as we all stand around Viv in front of the window. The light floats across her features beautifully, highlighting the dress we're holding up.

My fingers pinch the zipper, half way up, as we pose for another shot.

The camera clicks and flashes before the photographer looks down at it and then tells us she got the shot.

My heart hammers the closer we get to the wedding, but the buzz of champagne and the happiness clearly evident in everything Viv does is addictive.

I'm happy she's happy.

I want that happiness too.

"It's so beautiful on you," I tell Viv as I pull the zipper up and slip the fastener into place. "This dress looks like it was made for you." The lace and the deep V-neck, it's just stunning.

"My cheeks already hurt from smiling," Viv says teary-eyed. She's done a one-eighty in the last two hours. Ever since the crew started putting her dream wedding into place.

I had a dream wedding planned once. We'd been together for almost three years. It made sense to start thinking about church bells and all the white lace I could dream up.

Until Aiden broke my heart; twice.

The first time when he left me, volunteering to fight in the Army alongside his cousins and brother. Leaving me pining for him and worried every night of the two years he was gone. And bringing up memories I'd longed buried.

The second time was when he came back with his cousin in a casket and told me it was over. To stop sending him letters. I saw a broken man who needed love. He saw a way to hide in his regret, his pain, and even his anger.

I believe in true love and fate. And that's why I held on. He was the only one who knew me. Who really knew me.

In a world where I knew I didn't quite fit in, he was

my counter. My other half.

I let him come in and out of my life. Sneaking in late at night to hold me and fuck me, but never giving me anything other than pleasure in the dark.

The first night, I don't know if he was aware that I knew he'd come in.

I heard the door open, the creak stopped me from crying so hard. It was only days after the funeral. Days after he'd ended it, even though I'd sent him letters for years, and he'd sent them in return.

He wasn't going back to war; his time was over. But he wasn't coming back to me either.

I gave him a key and told him I knew why he didn't want to see me, but that it was okay. I was forever attached to a sin that he struggled to accept. But that didn't change how I felt about him, or how he felt about me.

He crept into the bedroom, as quiet as he could be. I still remember closing my eyes and pretending to sleep. I don't know how long he sat in the chair, but I know he cried quietly.

I gripped the comforter, wanting to go to him, but I knew that's not what he wanted. The next night it happened, I wouldn't let him cry alone. Even if he didn't want to tell me what'd happened.

Even though he let me hold him that night, it took days before he came back and when he did, he told me not to let anyone know. That night I cried with him, for both of us, but agreed to keep his secret.

The moment I did, he kissed me like he was starved for me. He whispered along the crook of my neck that he never wanted to see me in pain, that he never wanted to miss me again.

But he lied to me, he would miss me again. And I would miss him. Because he only came every so often, and we went about our lives separately, keeping up the rumors that after years of waiting for him to return, he broke my heart and left me.

Some would call it pathetic, that I would let a man come and go, not giving me anything other than his heart at night.

But secrets have layers that run deep. Just as he needed me, I needed him, and that's a truth no one can deny.

Chapter 4

Aiden

I've been waiting here for nearly half an hour, waiting for her to sneak out of the reception. The night air is crisp and sends a soothing chill up my jacket sleeves as I lean against the brick wall just outside of the back exit.

There's no one here as the sun sets along the trees of the forest behind the old brick building.

The crickets are louder than the music that drifts through the walls, and I know she could scream my name out here and none of them would hear it.

The door creaks open, the rusty hinges giving her away, my Ella, as she slips outside. Peeking up through her lashes, her hazel eyes are filled with nothing but desire.

"I thought you might be out here," she whispers and all I can do is watch her plump lips as she talks. I want them swollen like they are after a brutal kiss.

"I thought you'd never come," I tell her pushing off the wall.

"You lie," she whispers as I make my way to her, not bothering to wait for her to walk down the stairs. The steel steps clank as I walk up to her, wrapping my hands around her waist and pulling her in close to me.

"Never to you," I whisper against her lips before taking them. My fingers dig into the silk of her dress as I nip her lower lip and then groan at the sound of her moaning in my mouth.

"Tell me you're ready for me," I command her and then leave open-mouthed kisses down her neck. I bunch the fabric of her dress up as I move my way down her body.

"Here?" she gasps, although her fingers spear through my hair as I cup her pussy through the thin lace hiding it from me.

"Fuck." The word rumbles up my chest, my cock instantly hard. "I can feel how much you want me; you're so fucking wet." My body is on fire, every nerve ending springing to life knowing I'll have her soon.

"Aiden." My name on her lips is a plea as I push her back against the brick wall. I muffle her protests with a hard kiss.

I can feel her chest heave in a breath when I finally break the kiss and lift her legs to wrap around my waist. Her neck arches back as I trail my fingers up and down her cunt before hooking the lace with my thumb and shredding it. It tears easily and leaves her bared to me.

"I wish I had time to savor you," I confess at the dip in her throat as I shove her panties into my pocket so no evidence will be left behind.

"Tonight," she whispers reverently in the cool air as I unzip my pants and stroke myself.

The head of my cock slips between her lips and it feels like heaven. "I've waited for you all day," I tell her as rub my tip against her clit. She writhes against the wall, her eyes closed tightly and she silences her moans by sinking her teeth into her bottom lip.

"Look at me," I demand and instantly her hazel gaze pierces mine and I thrust into her in one motion, all the way to the hilt. Her legs tense around me, her mouth drops open into that beautiful 'O' and I stay buried deep inside of her tight cunt to let her adjust.

"Aiden," she whimpers as her nails dig in deeper, trying to pierce my skin even through my jacket.

"Ella," I breathe her name back to her in the hot air, lost in her gaze until I can thrust into her again.

Her back tries to arch against the wall and I have to grip her wrists, holding them above her head, so I can pin her where I want her. One hand on her hip, the other on her wrists, I fuck her ruthlessly against the brick wall.

Her cunt spasms without warning and my toes curl, my balls draw up, but I refuse to let go. Holding my breath, I watch her cum, the blush rising up her cheeks, and her chest rising and falling with her chaotic breathing.

"I love you," she whispers in the night air. All I've ever done is love her. It's myself I couldn't love for so long. How could I not have known?

"Where is it?" I ask her, needing to see it. I have to see it right now. I have to know it means to her what it does to me.

"My necklace," she gasps as I rock myself into her, brushing her clit as I do.

Pulling on the thin chain of her necklace, the rings appear on the end of it. The engagement ring and wedding band. The set that was my grandmother's and now belongs to her.

The wedding rings I didn't want anyone to see, but the rings I needed her to have. That night she left the party, I wanted to leave beside her. I needed her hand in mine and for everyone to see. Instead, I watched her walk away until she reached for the keys to her car.

I decided at the moment I saw her pause at her door, the keys jingling in her hand, that my place was beside her and I couldn't hide anymore. I'm not the only one with secrets, and I know if mine is ever known, it may bring up her own. Still, she deserves more than what I'd given her, she deserved every piece of me. After all, she already had every piece I could spare in her back pocket. So, I grabbed her hand and pulled her away, and married her that night.

I made the woman I've always loved my wife. The world has yet to see it, but tonight she'll leave with me.

The light shines on the platinum bands as they fall to her chest and I let go of her wrists, letting my hands roam back up her dress so I can fuck her savagely, taking what's mine.

Her heels dig into my ass and she kisses me frantically as I piston my hips. I cum with her and only break away after her breathing has calmed and she can bear to stand on her own. I watch her as she sags against the wall and she watches me.

She's mine. She's always been mine.

"I love you too," I finally tell her and lick my lower lip to kiss her one more time, before smoothing her dress back down and helping her to fix her hair.

"You're the one who said we should hide it," she reminds me as I slip the rings back into place, hidden beneath the neckline of her dress.

"You're the one who said it would be wrong to elope just before our best friends' wedding," I counter. I'm ready for the world to know again. They can't know what happened in between. I wish I could erase it all, but that will never happen.

Ella whispers, "I don't want to hide anymore." And for the first time in years, I think it's safe. I'm willing to risk it. I need her back in every way.

"Thank you for loving me," I tell her as my throat gets tight with emotion, remembering how she said 'I do' at the courthouse. "For never stopping sending me letters." The letters held it all together. I wouldn't have known that she truly loved me without them. That she could look past the pain just to hold on to me.

"I told you I'd love you through the war. I know sometimes it doesn't end just because you came home." Her bottom lip wobbles and I know why.

"You know it was more than that," I whisper to her. Only the second time I've dared to hint at the truth allowed. But it's Ella, and she knows it was all for her. I would do anything for her.

She never told me what my cousin had done to her, but she didn't have to. I could see it in her eyes that day.

He hurt her, so I hurt him back.

The Army taught me how to kill; love taught me the power of vengeance.

Burying my head in the crook of her neck, I hold on to Ella, wrapping my arms around her waist and pulling her small body into my chest.

"You know I love you. I could never stop loving you," she whispers.

"For the rest of my life, I'm yours."

Our love story is dark and twisted, haunted by a past we didn't choose. But it doesn't make it anything less than the purest of loves.

Epilogue

Ella

Some secrets are worth keeping. Just as is some love.

The day I found out who Aiden's cousin was, as they sat together ready to enlist, is the day everything changed between us. He was my only, my everything, for years before. And in my heart, my first.

I've never told anyone what his cousin did to me, except the night it happened, but Aiden knew without speaking the truth. I didn't tell him; I didn't think he'd believe me. The way no one else had. Drunk at a party and underage with college boys, I should have known better. That's what they said to me back then. I didn't want Aiden to look at me the same way.

And so I never said a word.

The moment I saw his cousin, I squeezed Aiden's hand and struggled to breathe as it all came back to me. I couldn't hide my fear and shame.

Aiden left that week, the look in his eye changed and that day, I thought everything would be ruined forever.

I had no idea what would happen, or the man Aiden would be when he came back. I never stopped writing him letters, or worrying that he'd stop loving me.

He didn't tell me what he'd done when he came home, but just as he knew my secret, I knew his when his cousin's casket was lowered to the ground.

Neither of us could voice them and these secrets separated us. Almost broke us.

He struggled with the pain of what'd happened to me, but also what he'd done. He stayed away, not wanting to risk what would happen to me if we were together when his secret came to life.

I remember how he whispered in the dark when he realized I knew, *"If they find out, I'll never tell why. Promise me, you'll let me take the fall and never speak a word."* When I promised him, I wouldn't say a thing, and I'd stay his secret until the case was closed, I made a promise to myself as well, to never lie to him again.

But they never found out. No one knows and now he's come back to me.

Love has a way of turning you into a person you never thought you could be.

It takes time and distance to recover. More than that, it takes love. I would never have stopped loving Aiden, before or after the war, before knowing how close our secrets were.

People wait for love.

People die for love.

People kill for love, too.

Some secrets are worth keeping. And I'll keep his secrets forever, just as he kept mine.

But after tonight, no more secrets. I want our love back, to be his and for everyone to know it, always and forever.

Bad Boy Next Door

Chapter 1

Ryker

My chopper slows, and I plant my foot down in the gravel. The crunch of my boot and the October breeze blowing against my face make me grin.

I'm a good distance away from the address the boys gave me, and I take a hard look at it.

This place is fucking insane. It's not a house. It's a mansion. The corner of my lips kick up into a grin. This is gonna be one hell of a party.

I've got this damn coat on for this party, but it's a bit too hot for it. I didn't have anything else to wear for the Halloween party. I'm not one for dressing up in costume, but I'm not gonna ruin the vibe of the party either. So this jacket means I'm a hunter. That's as dressed up as I'm getting.

I wasn't gonna come even though the boys all invited me. But then I heard Catherine was gonna be there. It's a college party, although it's at some mansion owned by two professors that are brothers. I wasn't invited by the professors directly, so I guess technically I'm crashing the party.

And I haven't laid eyes on Catherine since I took off. I moved out two years ago and never looked back. Leaving my shit parents behind and getting my life on track is exactly what I needed to do.

I huff a laugh as I kick my bike back to life and feel the vibrations under my ass. They made sure I knew I was nothing but trouble growing up. And that's exactly what I am, but I'll keep it to myself.

I've got a business to run now, and clients that fucking love my choppers. My parents can get fucked for all I care. I've moved on and accepted we'll never see eye to eye.

But that's not the part that sucked when I left.

It was not having my eyes on the good girl next door anymore. Catherine Parker. She's two years younger than me, and I never thought much of her as we grew up together, to be honest. Then one day, shortly after she turned seventeen, something shifted inside of me.

Suddenly she had curves where she didn't before. Her

tank top would ride up, and the only thing I wanted to do was pull it off and get a better look at her sun-kissed bare skin. I was nineteen though, so I kept my distance.

I'd also just gotten my job at the mechanic shop and started realizing what real life was, and how abusive my parents truly were. I wanted to get out, but I can't deny that knowing she was right next door kept me there longer than it should have.

The day I left she was outside on her porch as I grabbed the two boxes of stuff I owned and put them in the back of my buddy's car.

That was two years ago, and I didn't take the chance to make her mine. I should have, but she wasn't even eighteen yet. And I was almost twenty. Besides, I was no good for her. I truly believed that back then. I wanted to ravage her, ruin her for any other man. I wanted to make her mine.

I'd never felt that way before, and that fear of wanting to completely dominate her and own her kept me from taking her right then. I didn't want to destroy her. I didn't wanna bring her down to my level.

Times have changed though, and I wanna get a good look at Catherine now.

Jake and Levi know her from classes at the university. I'm making their custom bikes, and I happened to overhear her name. I know I'm not one of them. Shit, they're jocks, and I'm a mechanic. But we share the love of bikes and that gives them a good name in my book.

The wrench slipped right out of my hand as her name rolled off his lips. I've been working on bikes for nearly six years; it's what kept me out of trouble all those years ago. But hearing her name got me so worked up, I couldn't remember how to do a damn thing. Lucky for him she was just his study partner. If her name had been dropped in any other way... I'm not sure what I would've done.

Being reminded of her brought back all those memories. It brought back a sense of regret. But everything happens for a reason. I hadn't wanted to leave the way I did, but I had to get away from my parents. And now I'm a better man. I still wanna ruin her though. That shit hasn't changed.

Hearing her name made me work a little faster to get those bikes done and keep in touch with them.

They said she'd be here. I wasn't too subtle about asking how she's doing. I'm sure they know what's up, but that's good, because I want everyone to know.

I'm known for getting what I want even if I have to destroy everything in my path to get it. And I want her. I've waited too damn long.

I park my bike and stride toward the mansion with purpose. Tonight she's getting a taste of the bad boy next door.

Chapter 2

Catherine

I take another sip of champagne and lean against the wall of the dimly lit dining room. The music of the party is pumping, and the bass is making the walls vibrate slightly. I didn't have much to eat before I started drinking, and now I'm starting to get a buzz. I should be alright though. I had some of those pumpkin pie bites when I came in here.

I look over my shoulder to the foyer. I'm waiting. I've been waiting and staring at those damn doors ever since I got here. I feel slightly sick to my stomach with nerves. Maybe this buzz isn't from the alcohol at all.

I should be studying for my calculus test. I shouldn't

even be at this party. But I had to know if he was really going to come.

I heard Ryker's going to be here.

My parents warned me to stay away from him. He comes from bad blood, they said. But they don't see him the way I do. Still, I know he'd only want me for a night. I can't give in to those fantasies. He's never wanted me anyway.

One of the football guys said he's coming. I've been helping Levi in class. I don't mind being his study partner. But when he started talking about Ryker Dean I swear I couldn't focus on anything else. I'm supposed to be Levi's study partner, but when we get together all I wanna do is ask about what Ryker's been up to. I can't believe he's got his own business now. He always loved motorcycles. I'm so fucking happy for him. But my heart still hurts.

He left me years ago and never said a damn word. It's not like I was entitled to even a simple goodbye, but it broke something inside of me when he left.

I feel pathetic for being so worked up over hearing his name. I'm no one to him. I should know better by now. I know all too well that men are assholes.

I take a deep breath and settle myself down. Not all men are assholes, and just because Ryker left doesn't make him an asshole.

After all, I would've left too if I had his parents. It hurts my heart to think about everything he went through. He was right there, right next door. I could hear them yelling all the time. It wasn't right. That's what my mom used to say. A few times she wanted to go over there, but Dad held her back.

He'd had words with Ryker's father more than a time or two. It put a stop to some of it, but not for long. Words weren't enough. Even calling the police when we heard them fighting didn't do a thing.

I clear my throat, trying to shut down the bad memories. I'm glad Ryker left. He didn't deserve that.

Maybe that's why I've felt like my heart belongs to Ryker. In a lot of ways, it does. I was right there hurting for him, but I couldn't do anything. I was just a girl. I wish I had been stronger. I wish I could've gone over there and stopped his parents from beating on him and saying all those awful things to him.

"Whatever mood you're in," Khloe begins, interrupting my thoughts as she points the cigarette holder in my face, "Knock it out." I stare back at her and bite my tongue.

She's wearing *my* costume. I wanted to be Audrey Hepburn. I was the one who bought that costume. I should've said no when she asked to wear it. She does this shit all the time. She twirls the pearls around her finger, *my pearls*, and purses her lips. "Come on. We're here to get drunk and get laid. And no one's going to come around us with that sad look on your face."

She tilts the champagne flute in my hand up toward my mouth. "Drink up!"

I got stuck with a shit roommate. A really shitty roommate. Next semester I'm moving out. She's so selfish, and somehow she always convinces me to give her whatever she wants.

I have to live with her, so I don't want to rock the boat. I'll just deal with this shit for one more month. One and a half, to be precise.

I throw back the small glass of champagne.

It's actually really good. And at least Khloe got me thinking about something else for a change. I don't need to think about Ryker or anything else other than relaxing tonight.

Just as the thought enters my head, I look over to the doors and see him standing there.

My lips part and I have to bite down on the inside of my cheek as my eyes travel over his masculine body.

Ryker looks different from when I saw him last, but in the best of ways.

He's taller, and his shoulders are broader and more built. He shrugs off the camo jacket he's wearing, and his clean white t-shirt is snug around his frame and thick biceps.

He runs a hand through his dark hair and and walks over to Levi and the other guys hanging around the table plated up with hors d'oeuvres. I was munching on them earlier. Liam and Marcel really went all out. It's a bit odd calling the Henderson professors by their first names. It's strange even being here for this party. But I fucking love it. It's thrilling to get out and have some fun.

I need to do this more often. But large parties just aren't my scene.

I hear Ryker's deep rough laugh as someone jokes about him coming in costume.

He shrugs his shoulders with a sexy grin on his face. "I'm a hunter." Hearing his voice again after all these years makes my heart skip a beat in my chest and my pussy heat with anticipation.

"What the fuck is he doing here?" Khloe spits out. I cringe just hearing her voice.

Ryker's head whips over to us just as I turn to tell her off.

My body freezes as I feel his eyes on me.

I feel like a nervous little girl all over again. I nervously try to pull my long hair into a ponytail. It's a stupid habit I have, but I forgot I'm wearing a damn headband with bunny ears, and it slips down off my head and over my eyes.

Stupid fucking ears.

I curse under my breath and try to compose myself

as Khloe laughs.

I was a rabbit last year. I felt so cute. The ears are white, and I had a cute white dress with a puff on the butt for my bunny tail. I did my own makeup, all cute with little dots and whiskers.

But I spilled something on the dress, staining it at the end of the night last year.

And since Khloe came to me last minute, crying about not having a costume, I'm just in a white tank top and jeans. I don't even have a cute little puff on the butt. I just pulled these ears out of the back of the closet instead of getting a new pair. She should've been the damn bunny.

I did put some pink lipstick on the tip of my nose and drew whiskers on my face using eyeliner. But I don't feel nearly as pretty in this getup compared to last year's.

My cheeks heat with a blush. He's going to see me like this.

My fingers fly to my face to check if my makeup's okay. Which is stupid as fuck, 'cause as I look down at my fingertips which are now covered in black eyeliner, I'm sure all I did was smudge it.

I need to get to a bathroom ASAP. Khloe starts to say something while rolling her eyes, but I ignore her and head straight to the kitchen. I know there's a bathroom nearby.

As I walk away from her, I hear Levi call out my name. My blood heats, and I almost trip in these heels. No way. I am not going over there like this. It's been years since I've seen Ryker, and I need to make sure I don't look like a mess. Even if that's what I feel I am right now.

I keep walking straight ahead and pretend like I don't hear him. I don't stop until I reach the bathroom, quickly closing the door and leaning against it, sagging in relief. Holy shit.

He's really here. A broad smile covers my face as I push off the door and go right to the mirror. I slide the strap of my clutch off my wrist and pull out my eyeliner.

This is gonna be an easy fix.

I breathe out deeply and shake out my nerves. The smile on my face won't go away. I'm finally going to put my big girl panties on and make sure Ryker knows exactly how I feel about him.

Chapter 3

Ryker

My heartbeats feel like weak flickers in my chest. I know she saw me. I fucking know she did. And what'd she do? She turned and walked away as fast as she fucking could.

Maybe I'm remembering all this wrong. I thought she was into me back then.

Maybe she's pissed. After all, I did up and leave without saying a damn word to her. Maybe she's just grown up and realized I'm not good for her.

That thought fucking hurts. Mostly because it's true.

When we were younger, I used to help her get through the woods in the back of our development. I knew I couldn't have her, but whenever she asked me for help, I couldn't say no.

She wanted a shortcut to the strip mall right behind the woods. So I made one for her. It took a few days, but I made her a nice little path. She was too scared to go by herself, and I used to hang out at the mall anyway, so I didn't mind escorting her. I used to wait for her to come knock on our back door during the week. My parents were hardly ever home until later in the day. Much later. And she was so predictable, coming by every day at four.

If my parents were home, she'd come out her back door late at night and throw rocks at my window to get my attention. She'd ask all sweet and shy if I was gonna go with her the next time she planned on making a trek. She always apologized. She never got over that, even the last time we went. I remember how she looked up at me with vulnerability in her eyes, expecting me to be annoyed or just say no.

I never did. I would never tell her no.

She was so fucking cute. If only she knew how much I looked forward to seeing her.

It was a guilty pleasure of mine. I knew I could never have her. She was too sweet and innocent, and I was just a lowlife who'd never amount to anything.

But I could at least enjoy her company and pretend like there was more between us.

That was years ago, and back then she didn't know any better.

She should know better now than to let me have a taste of her. My heart plummets in my chest, all the way down to my stomach. She does know better. That has to be why she walked away.

I don't realize I'm staring until Levi shoves a beer in my hand. It's ice cold, and the condensation on the outside of the bottle almost makes it slip from my grasp.

The guys are all looking at me, and I wanna smack the shit out of them.

"What?" I ask in a hard voice.

"Guess she didn't hear me," Levi says and shrugs. She heard him. Just like I heard that chick with the pearls ask what I was doing here. I think I recognize her from somewhere, but I can't place her. Maybe she was friends with Catherine back when I used to live next door. I don't remember any of her friends being like that toward me back then, but that chick in the pearls sure as fuck doesn't like me now.

This was a fucking waste of time. I shouldn't be here trying to blend in when I don't belong.

I open my mouth to come up with some excuse to bail, but Jake throws his arm around my shoulders. He's got his fake vampire teeth in his mouth, and it keeps throwing me off every time he smiles.

"She just went to powder her nose." His breath smells like beer as he leans into me and laughs. At first I'm pissed they're having a good laugh about it, but then he adds, "You gotta tell him what she said, Levi."

My heart does that stupid nervous shit again and I take a drink of my beer with my eyes on Levi. Jake chuckles and pats my back hard as I bring my arm back down. I don't want them to know how on edge I am. But damn, I really am sweating this.

I didn't realize how much I wanted her until right now. Until the idea that she didn't want me back popped into my head. I fucking hope that's not the case. I want her.

Levi's grin spreads across his face. "Dude, she fucking *wants* you."

"She said that?" The words spill out of my mouth, and I can't help it. They come out fast, and the guys have a good laugh over it. I let out a sigh and turn my head back to look to where she left the dining room.

Levi looks me dead in the eyes and says, "Fuck no. You think she'd just come out and say it?"

I huff and let the irritation grow on my face.

"Relax, bro. She *wants* you." Jake draws out the word and I just stare back at him.

"If you're fucking with me, I'm gonna beat the shit out of you," I say, deadpan.

Jake pats my shoulder and urges, "Go get her, man. I

can't fucking stand the fact I lost the bet."

My blood heats, and I resist the urge to clench my fists. They made a bet about my girl?

"He bet that you'd be fucking her in a bathroom by now," Levi says with a grin.

"I knew you'd be classy and at least talk to her first," Mickey says to my left. This guy barely knows me, but at least he thinks I'm classy.

"It's so damn obvious you two want each other. Just go get her already." Levi's got a grin plastered on his face as he waits for me to respond. *Just go get her.* Like it's that easy. He must see the hesitation on my face.

"Will you two shut the fuck up if I go talk to her?" I ask them.

They all laugh and a smile finally cracks on my face. She wants me. Alright, I'm gonna go find her and get the girl I've wanted for so long. I down the rest of my beer and pass the empty bottle to Levi. He takes it and nods toward the dining room, which leads to the kitchen.

"Yeah, yeah, I know where she went."

Levi reaches his hand out to Jake, and Jake shakes his head. "No, we gotta make sure he gets laid, or you don't get paid." I chuckle as they get into it and take my leave.

As I make my way to the kitchen where Catherine went, a cute little cheerleader with glasses walks by. I look back over my shoulder at the guys as the argument ceases and they fall quiet. Jake's eyes are all over that ass. Those assholes can make fun of me all day, but I know they're just as caught up in getting their girls as I am.

Chapter 4

Catherine

I get only two steps out of the bathroom when my heart stops at a voice behind me.

"Did you really come here as a kitten?" I recognize Ryker's voice instantly, and it does things to my lower regions I'm ashamed to admit.

I turn with my clutch held tightly in my hand. My heart swells in my chest. I give him a small smile, and feel a blush rise to my cheeks. It's almost like time hasn't passed. He's leaning against the wall and kicks off it, shoving his hands in his pockets before he walks over to me.

I try to remember what he asked and when I do, I roll my eyes and say, "I'm a bunny." I point to the ears.

They're long and look nothing like cat ears. I love how it feels like we're just picking up where we left off though. It feels so natural talking to him. A stupid little voice that gives me false hope is screaming, *It's a sign! It's a sign!* I'm trying to shut it down, but I can't.

He huffs a small laugh. "I'm a hunter. I think you're in dangerous territory."

I scoff at him. "A cameo jacket makes you a hunter?" I involuntarily roll my eyes. Men hate this holiday.

He cocks a brow. "You do like to roll your eyes at me, don't you?" he asks in a low, threatening voice. It's a voice that would send shivers of fear through most people, but not to me. I know who he really is.

When we were younger and in his backyard, I saw his true colors. I saw him change into the bad boy everyone thinks he is at a moment's notice. Like he was putting on a facade.

Once I'd dropped an entire box of decorations for my parents' anniversary. A few tissue paper pompoms I wanted to hang from the deck blew over into the neighbor's yard, into his yard.

I was only fourteen at the time and he was a few years older, but I wanted him to notice me. My hormones were in full swing, as were the pimples on my face. And my mother wouldn't let me wear makeup. I cringe, remembering that fact about my childhood. How could

I not want him though? He had a motorcycle, and his right arm was covered with tattoos. He'd clean up the weeds in their front yard without his shirt on, and those lean muscles and deep "V" at his hips made him the star of my dreams at night.

He never looked my way though, not that I expected him to. Of course he wouldn't have. I was the pimply, naïve girl next door. But that day he was out back with low-hung jeans and a tight white t-shirt that fit snugly over his broad shoulders. And my mom's pink tissue pompom flew right over to him.

My heart stopped in my chest as he bent down with his muscles rippling and picked it up, raising one brow and looking at me with the corner of his lips kicked up into a smirk.

I apologized and nervously tucked my dirty blonde hair behind my ear. I'm sure I was blushing, for no good reason other than I was thinking naughty things I knew I shouldn't have been.

He just chuckled and offered to help me decorate. 'Cause that's the kind of guy he is.

I remember that day just like yesterday.

I wasn't tall enough to reach the deck, so he helped me. I just sat on the concrete porch and watched the sweat glisten on his sun-kissed body. I felt like a pervert creeping on him, but he didn't look at me like that. No matter how much I wanted him to.

And then my father came outside.

In an instant, Ryker's features went sharp and dark as my dad bitched him out. He told him to get out, and stay out. I was mortified. He was only helping me. My heart tried to climb up my throat, and I didn't say anything. I felt like a traitor. Like I'd betrayed him.

Ryker dropped the pompom and shrugged like he didn't care. But I could see it in his eyes. It was wrong. I cried my eyes out and yelled at my dad after he'd left, but the damage was done.

I'll never understand how my father could talk to him like that when he knew just as well as I did the shit his parents put him through. But then again, my dad yelled at me, too. He said I should know better. I wasn't allowed to date boys, and especially not THAT boy. I knew what I'd done was wrong. But Ryker hadn't done a damn thing wrong. That was years ago, and he's definitely not a bad boy... he's a bad man now. Or at least that's how he looks.

I know he's still the same at heart. Even if he doesn't look the part.

"I do like rolling my eyes at you," I say back in a flirty voice. Normally I'd be embarrassed by how apparent it is that I'm into him. But I've got a nice buzz going on now. It's not like he'd ever make a move on me anyway. A waiter passes us with a fresh tray of champagne glasses, and I snag one off of it. I give him a small smile and clutch onto the drink for dear life.

I need liquid courage.

"I like to see you get all wound up," I say in a lowered voice, looking up through my thick lashes. I'm going all in. I hope it came out as sexy as I think it did.

Ryker's eyes heat and narrow as he tries to hold my gaze. I slowly lick my lips and bite down on the bottom one. It does exactly what I'd hoped it would. His eyes focus in on my mouth and I can practically see his dick jump in his pants.

Yeah, I'm not a pimply little girl anymore. Look at me now, Ryker.

"Careful what you're doing, kitten. You're gonna get in trouble." He takes a step forward and part of me wants to instinctively step back. He's trouble with a capital T. But that's not happening tonight. I take a step forward, closing in a bit more. I could reach out and run my hands down his muscular chest if I wanted to. Well, I do want to. My pussy clenches around nothing.

"I told you, I'm a bunny, not a cat." I shake my head and slowly bring my drink to my lips. I don't even taste it as I take a swallow and keep my eyes on his the entire time. "You should listen to me sometime, Ryker."

"That's not why I'm calling you kitten. And you

should watch that mouth. You're really," he says as his large body cages me in, "gonna get your ass in trouble talking to me like that."

"By who? My dad's not here, Ryker." I surprise myself with how seductive my voice comes out. I must be *really* buzzed.

Ryker takes another step closer to me, and now we're so close we're only a few inches apart. He lowers his head and drops his lips down to my ear. His breath is hot against my neck, sending shivers down my spine. I close my eyes and tilt my head slightly. This is a fucking dream come true.

My heartbeat slows, and my lungs fill with his masculine scent.

But before the words fall from his lips, I hear a voice and my eyes pop open.

"Get away from her!" Khloe shrieks.

Chapter 5

Ryker

"What the fuck, Khloe?!" Catherine yells back at the bitch in the pearls. I take a step back as Khloe grips Catherine's arm and yanks her away from me. Catherine's drink spills and splashes on my jeans and the floor. She looks back at her friend with pure rage on her face.

My heart beats frantically, and I resist the urge to pull Catherine back to me.

She's *mine*.

In my head she is, but in reality, I have no claim on her. And she sure isn't the sweet little thing next door anymore. The years apart have only made her more beautiful, and confident, and brazen.

I fucking love it.

The chick tries to pull Catherine away even though my kitten is fighting it.

They're talking in angry whispers, and Khloe pulls her farther away from me, trying to get her out of earshot.

Catherine rips her arm from her friend's grip and looks back at her with disgust.

"Get away from him!" Khloe says loud enough for me to hear. Khloe's eyes keep darting from me to her, but Catherine's focused on her friend.

"What are you thinking?" Khloe screeches.

I barely hear Catherine reply. "What are you doing?" she practically hisses.

"A guy like that is a lowlife thug. He's the type of guy you fuck for a night, and then you're done." Catherine's eyes go wide. I take in a slow breath and try to let the fact that she doesn't defend me roll off my shoulders. But I'd be lying if I said I was successful.

"You deserve so much better than that prick. He may be good for one lay, but you'd feel like shit afterward." Catherine turns her body slightly, rocking on her heels and says something I can't hear. "Trust me, I'm saving you."

There's a pause for a long moment while Khloe rubs Catherine's back, like she's consoling her. I start to get this sick feeling in the pit of my stomach. Like that's really what Catherine wanted. Like she's upset because Khloe is just trying to talk her out of making a mistake.

Mistake. Yeah, that's what I am.

"He doesn't belong here." She scrunches her nose and points a fake cigarette in my direction. "I don't know who invited him, but he needs to leave. Now."

I watch as Catherine's mouth opens wide and she stares at her friend. I wait for an entire minute, and it feels like a lifetime. I wait for something, anything. But Catherine says nothing. Instead she slowly closes her mouth and crosses her arms across her chest, then looks past Khloe's shoulder and away from me.

It's like a bullet to my fucking chest.

Catherine isn't a girl you fuck for a night. She's the kinda girl you keep. I always knew that. And somewhere in me, I knew I wanted to keep her.

But I know what she was thinking. She just wanted to go slumming for the night.

I don't say a word; I turn on my heel and walk out.

The music is blaring in my ears. My shoulder bumps into the streamers hanging from the ceiling and they stick to my shoulder, irritating the fuck out of me. I rip them down and let them drift to the ground as I head to the door.

I walk past groups of people talking and laughing in corners. A few girls are dancing and squealing with laughter. Jake's climbing the spiral staircase, holding hands with the cheerleader I saw earlier..

Fuck. I don't belong here.

As I turn the doorknob and open the door slightly, Levi's hand comes out and slams it shut. Fucker's about to get punched in the face.

"What the fuck, man?" Levi asks.

I keep my teeth clenched to prevent me from saying something I can't take back to a client. That's all he is. I was fucking stupid to try to make friends with him or any of them in here.

I was perfectly fine burying myself in work and staying out of trouble. Right now all I wanna do is pick a fight, and Levi's about to figure that out if he doesn't back off.

"What happened?" Levi asks with some hesitation in his voice. He's searching my face for something, but I don't answer. I'm not fucking telling him.

I'm angry. My body is screaming at me to lash out. To just take my anger out on him. But more than that, I'm hurt, and I don't wanna show it.

"Are you alright?" he asks. And that's the last fucking straw.

"Get off the fucking door," I say through gritted teeth and pray he does it. 'Cause if not, my hand's coming off the knob and my fist is slamming into his face.

I pull on the doorknob and he takes his hand off of it, letting the door open wide enough for me to get out.

I don't look back at him, and he lets me go without further fuss. Good move on his part. I walk across the grass rather than taking the path. I make a beeline right for where I left my bike.

I need to get the fuck out of here, and never look back.

It's better it happened this way. I was a fucking idiot to think I'd ever be anything to her. I still have my tats. I'm a Dean. I have my asshole parents' blood in me. I'll never be good. I'll never be worth anything.

It was stupid to think I'd be good enough for her.

I kick my bike to life and take off. I don't bother to look back even when I hear Catherine calling out my name.

Chapter 6

Catherine

I can't believe what this bitch is saying. I can't even look at her. And now she's talking about him the same way his parents did. All the memories flood back at once. I feel weak and helpless listening to the way his own mother used to talk to him. I cross my arms over my chest and turn away while tears run down my cheeks. I force myself to breathe out deeply.

I'm taken back to a night when we came home together. He'd always wait for me at the food court when the mall had curfew. He knew I didn't like walking in the woods alone. Especially at night.

We walked mostly in silence. I had a cherry slushie,

and I have no idea why because it was so damn cold outside. He laughed at me when I started shivering and took off his Henley. I remember how we stopped on the edge of the woods. The moon was out and it was bright. I could see all of his lean muscle and that "V" at his hips I used to dream about.

He handed it to me to cover myself with. I wore a thin tank top that cut off at my midsection. I'd worn it for him of course. I always made sure I looked cute if I was going to be around him. I was always hoping he would notice me.

I had to try hard to keep myself from looking at his body, and judging from the smirk on his face, he knew that. I remember how hot I felt then. I was a bundle of nerves and embarrassed for being caught looking. I expected him to make fun of me or put me in my place, but instead he just walked into the woods like normal.

He always walked faster than me, maybe because he's taller? But I remember he seemed to be walking faster than normal that night. I kept telling myself it was because he was cold. I offered a few times to give him his shirt back, but he insisted I wear it. It was obvious he just wanted to get home and get away from me. At least that's what I thought until I tripped over a tree root. I would've landed hard on my face. The damn slushie went flying and splattered on the ground.

I let out a shriek and prepared to fall in the dirt and land hard on the ground, but he caught me. Both of his strong arms wrapped around my waist and pulled me up until I was pressed against his hard chest.

I thought he was going to kiss me. My hands were on his bare chest, and the way he was holding me close made every nerve ending in my body burst into flames.

I remember how my breathing came in pants and I swear that even in the darkness I saw a heat in his eyes. But in a flash it was gone, like I'd just imagined it. And he set me down on my feet, leaving me confused and shaken.

He slowed his pace, and we walked home in silence. And it was an awkward silence. I kept my hands clasped to keep me from reaching out to him.

I felt fucking nauseated and practically ran to my house. I always entered through the back door so my father wouldn't see I'd walked through the woods with Ryker. He was my dirty little secret. My parents would have killed me.

That night when I walked in, I'd completely forgotten I was wearing his Henley. I walked right in without thinking.

I was bombarded with questions. I wasn't allowed to date anyone, and my father said it was unacceptable for me to be around Ryker, even if he was just a friend. He was in the middle of scolding me when we heard the neighbors.

Ryker's parents were having a fight. It wasn't obvious at first. But then there was a loud yell of pain. I think his dad hit his mom. And then Ryker got in the middle. He always did that. He always defended his mom, even when she was the one yelling at him half the time.

The way Khloe is talking about Ryker reminds me of Mrs. Dean. It makes me want to slam my fist in her face.

I finally snap out of my recollection and look that bitch in the eyes.

"Fuck you." That's all I give her as I turn around and go back to where I left Ryker. But he's not there.

I walk quickly around the corner searching for him, but I don't know where he went. My heart races with worry. He left me? Fucking Khloe ruined it for me. Oh my god, what if he heard her?

"What the--" Khloe sneers as she puts her hand on my bare shoulder, digging her nails in so I'm forced to turn around. I don't even think about it as I clench a fist and punch her right in her face.

She lets out a wail and clutches at her nose with her hands.

My eyes go large. Holy fuck!

I can't believe I hit her. I mean, I've dreamed of doing it for so long. She's definitely had it coming. But still. Holy hell.

She's bent over, but then she stands and pulls her

hands away from her face. There's no blood, but her face is all red, and her nose is starting to swell.

"You bitch!" she yells out, her eyes glassy with tears. I start to feel bad, but then I remember what she said about Ryker.

"You fucking had it coming." I almost leave but then I think to add, "Don't you ever talk about him like that again." As if she'll listen to me. I know she won't and there's going to be hell to pay for this, but I don't care. What she said is not okay, and I'm not going to pretend like it is.

She looks up at me with complete disgust and opens her mouth to say something. But two drunk girls come into the room and one doesn't see Khloe clutching her nose.

She tumbles right over her and they fall into a pile on the floor. There's yelling and pushing, and the other drunk girl is just staring wide-eyed.

I have no intention of staying to see the end of this. I head to the ballroom where everyone else has been hanging out. The music gets louder as I approach, and the lights are flickering in beat with the music.

I look all over, and each second that passes my heart slams harder in my chest.

He had to have heard. For a fleeting second I think maybe he was bored and is making out with someone in a corner. But I push those thoughts aside.

There's a reason I feel the way I do about him. The way he held me all those years ago did something to me. I know it did. Tears prick my eyes and they make me feel weak. I am not going to cry. I am going to find him, and I'm going to beat his ass for leaving me like that.

I nod my head as I leave the ballroom and see Levi by the door. I pick up my pace to ask him if he's seen Ryker, but I slow down when I get close and see his expression.

He looks pissed. I come to a halt as he walks toward me.

"What happened?" His voice is hard, and it's a demand. I don't like it. I don't like being talked to that way. I'm cool with Levi, but he better watch it.

"I don't like the way you're talking to me, and where's Ryker?" I say coolly.

Levi's brow scrunches, and his hard features soften.

"He took off."

My heart plummets, and my throat closes. He left me again. That fucking bastard. I bite down on the inside of my cheek to keep from crying.

"What happened?" he asks again.

"Khloe's a bitch. That's what happened."

Levi stares at me for a second before moving aside. "He just left, so maybe you can catch him."

A small bit of hope blooms in my chest. I race to the

door and open it just in time to see Ryker on his bike taking off. I call out for him, but he doesn't hear.

I stand in the open doorway and watch him grow smaller in the distance.

Motherfucker. I'm so angry and hurt and upset.

I take a deep breath, trying to calm myself and grip the door harder so I don't slam it over and over again like I want to out of frustration.

I'm just going to leave. I don't need this shit right now.

If he really wanted me, he knows where to find me, I think as I step outside and walk to the garage. But then I stop cold in my tracks and remember that Khloe drove. Looks like I'm walking home.

I unzip my clutch to make sure I have my keycard to the dorm. I do, but I don't want to go back there. I don't want to deal with her. For all I know she called the cops on me. It sounds like something she'd do.

I zip it shut and just start walking. I'll figure something out on the way.

I walk down the long, winding driveway and onto a busier road with street lights. It's a little chilly, but still warm considering the time of year. There's a permanent frown on my face that I just can't stop making. I hate that this part of the road is empty, but farther down there are more houses and a development. I try to walk quickly, but I don't want to. I don't have the energy, and

I'm sure as hell not in a race to get home.

I didn't really want to go to that party anyway. I just wanted to see him, and I was too scared to go to the shop. I waited for him to come to me, and I can do that again.

I wrap my arms around my chest and rub my forearms to heat them up.

That's not going to happen. I already know it. He left me before, and now he's doing it all over again. If I want to see him, I'm going to have to go to him.

How pathetic. I feel so damn pathetic. I'm like some lovesick child who can't get over her crush who's probably not even into me.

My eyes go glassy and I don't care. The hot tears run down my face and I angrily wipe them away.

He was going to kiss me though. I know he was. But for him it was probably something else. A one-time fuck.

It hurts to think that, but it's true. I know it is.

I wipe my face again and look down at my hands. Shit, I forgot about the makeup. My hands are covered in black eyeliner with a smear of bright pink lipstick.

I quickly hunch over and scrub my face with the bottom of my tank top, feeling a cool breeze blow across my midsection as I angrily rub off as much as I can. As I do, the bunny ears slide down my face and I rip them off and throw them on the ground like a petulant child.

I stare at them for a second and decide to pick them

up. I can't just leave them on the side of the road, even if right now I hate them. I see a trash can on the side of someone's house and walk quickly to it to throw tonight's offending evidence in the bin. Now it's right where it belongs.

I take in a staggering breath and keep walking. I have a good twenty to thirty-minute walk ahead of me still. But I need it. I must look like a mess. I'm sure my face is red and puffy from rubbing at it. My hair is all tangled, and I don't even have a hair tie to pull it back like I want to.

I hear trick-or-treaters squealing as they run on the sidewalk across the street. They're going in the opposite direction, and their parents are behind them chatting while the kids run ahead.

I look like a wreck, and I feel pathetic and disappointed with everything.

I just need to sleep, but I don't want to go back to the dorms.

Fate doesn't care about what I want though. That much is obvious.

She brought Ryker into my life again, only to dangle him in front of me one last time before snatching him from my grasp.

Fate's a bitch.

I close my eyes and shake my head. No, it's my fault. It was my fault back then for not doing everything

I could to help him. And it's my fault tonight for not pushing Khloe away faster and leaving with him. I wish I'd seen him go. I would've gone with him.

Fate gave me a second chance, and I blew it. That's no one's fault but my own.

Chapter 7

Ryker

I can't fucking run away every time I get pissed. But running is better than snapping. I can't afford to let my temper get me into trouble. My mouth is still slammed shut. I slow down as I approach a red light and look down at my hands to examine them. It's a habit of mine that helps me calm down. There's usually oil somewhere around my fingernails even if I scrub them clean. I don't see anything though.

I look over to my left at the kids in their little fairy and skeleton costumes screeching with delight, and then to my right at a 24/7 convenience store and gas station. I shouldn't be driving right now, not in this state. I just need to calm down for a minute. I pull in and park my bike, but I don't get off.

I'm not very good with conflict. I'm better than I used to be. Back then it was fight, fight, fight. Not that I wanted to fight that bitch.

I don't know what her problem was. It's been years since someone's talked to me like that. It still fucking hurts though. It wasn't even to my face, but at least it wasn't behind my back.

I thought I'd changed. I *have* changed. I know I have. I'm good enough for her. But either Catherine can't see it, or she doesn't want to.

He needs to leave now. I remember Khloe's words and they get me all pissed off again. That's when the memories hit me. Khloe's the chick who was dating that IT guy I hired.

I groan and cover my face with my hands.

Her being a bitch tonight is definitely because of me, but it has nothing to do with who I am.

She came into the office of my shop awhile back. I knew she was with him. I think his name was Joey. I can't even remember. I only hired him for a week to set up the new system. She came in at lunch to see him every day. And each passing day she showed me more and more attention. So much so that I felt bad for the guy.

And then she came into my office and closed the door

behind her. I can't remember what she said verbatim, but she basically offered me a quick fuck.

All I said to her was, *You can leave now unless you want me to call your boyfriend in here and repeat what you just said.* I never saw her again. Not that I minded. But now her little rant makes sense.

A smile creeps up on my face. She's just holding a grudge and jealous I was giving Catherine attention.

I feel a small bit of relief, but only for a moment.

Catherine's gonna be pissed at me for leaving maybe. But she still didn't stick up for me.

That's what really matters. She could have, but she didn't.

She turned me down. Well technically she didn't, since I never even asked.

I went there to finally get the girl I've been lusting after. The girl I've been working hard to be good enough for. It's been two years, but I've been working steadily toward that goal. And as soon as it got rough, I walked away.

Fuck. I run a hand down my face. I can't believe I fucked this up.

My forehead pinches and I kick my bike back to life. The loud rumble fills the air as I make a left out of the gas station and head back to the party.

I'm tired of not being good enough. I want her.

I'm going to make sure she knows it.

As determination sets in and I rev my bike up, I almost crash the damn thing.

Catherine's alone and on the left side of the road. Her arms are crossed like she's cold, and she looks upset.

My heart sinks in my chest. What happened?

I have to wait to make a U-turn at the next light and pull up behind her.

I left her, again.

I need to make sure she forgives me. I need to make this right and most importantly, I need to get my girl.

Chapter 8

Catherine

I hear the dull roar of a motorcycle, and I have to close my eyes and push out the image of Ryker on his bike. I don't think I'll ever not see him when I hear a motorcycle.

The rumble gets closer and closer, but then softer as whoever it is pulls up close to me.

My heart thuds in my chest, and suddenly I'm scared I'm here alone at night.

This is a good area of town, but crime happens everywhere. I'm too scared to even turn around as I walk quicker and closer to the edge of the sidewalk. But then I hear his voice.

"You need a ride."

My head whips around at the sound, and I stand dumbfounded.

"Ryker?" My blood heats, and anxiety washes through me. I take several steps closer to him, gripping my clutch tight in my hands.

My blood surges with adrenaline, and the exhaustion that was weighing me down before vanishes.

Fate gave me another chance. I can't blow it.

I walk to his bike and prepare to just put it all out there. Taking a deep breath, I say, "Ryker, I'm sorry."

"Catherine, I'm sorry," he says at the same time as me.

My breath stops, and my mouth opens slightly. I don't know what he could possibly be sorry for. He looks at me as though he's thinking the same thing.

He throws a leg over his bike and walks in front of me. A car's coming, but we're safe here on the sidewalk. He looks over his shoulder as the car drives by and watches as it drives away.

He takes a step closer, looking me in the eyes. I know how I must look; I'm a mess and I hate that, but all I see in his eyes is desire. It's like that night all over again.

He starts to talk, but I don't want to hear it.

I don't know if it's the exhaustion, the thought of losing him again, or the fact that he came to get me when I was so down on myself, but something pushes me to wrap my arms around his neck, get on my tiptoes and push my lips against his.

I kiss him with the desperation I feel. I can't lose him again. I can't let him leave again without him knowing exactly how much he means to me.

I catch him by surprise, and at first his lips are hard. Then they soften and mold to mine. His hand splays across my lower back. My tank top has ridden up some, and the feel of his warm hands on my bare skin is heaven. He pulls me closer to him as his other hand cups the back of my head, angling my head so he can kiss me back passionately.

I keep my eyes closed and moan into his mouth. My body arches of its own accord and my pussy heats for him.

I've waited years just for this kiss, but it isn't enough. I want more.

As the sound of another car approaching barely registers, Ryker breaks the kiss and moves us backward and onto the sidewalk.

He looks down at me with his chest rising and falling, and lust in his eyes.

My lips feel slightly swollen from his bruising kiss.

"You need a ride?" he asks in a low voice.

I start to answer, but then my eyes fall. I clear my throat. I don't want to go back to the dorm. I don't want him to just drop me off.

But I'm not going to tell him no.

"What's wrong?" he asks, searching my eyes before I can even answer. He cups my chin in his hand and forces me to look at him.

"I just want to go home with you tonight." I say each word slowly and carefully. My heart races in my chest.

I've never gone home with a man. I've never done anything with a man beyond kissing. And even then, it was nothing like what I just had with Ryker.

Ryker cocks an eyebrow and an asymmetric grin pulls his lips up.

He leans down and quickly plants a kiss on my lips.

"I'm not gonna say no to that, kitten." His rough voice sparks the desire in my core once again. My heart flutters in my chest as he reaches behind him and grabs a helmet off the back of his bike.

Chapter 9

Ryker

I rev the engine a little more as we get closer. Catherine lets out a small squeal of delight, and her arms squeeze me tighter.

Her cheek is pressed against my back, and it's everything I thought it'd be.

We ride in silence as her warmth molds to my back and her arms hug my waist.

As we pull up to a red light, her hands slip down lower. She starts to slide them past the waistband and down farther. Her fingertips tickle my pelvis, and my dick jumps.

Fuck, I need to control myself. I wanna get off this

bike and bend her ass over. She'd have it coming to her, teasing me like this. Instead I grip her wrist and put her hand back where it should be.

"You're going to have to wait, kitten," I tell her over my shoulder. I watch as she gives me a sexy little pout.

Now my dick is hard, and my girl is horny. Thank fuck my place is right around the corner. I can't wait any longer.

She's a good girl the rest of the way, but feeling her body pressed against mine and knowing she wants me has made my dick impossibly hard. Fucking her tight pussy is all I can think about as I pull up and climb off as quick as I can.

I help her off the bike, making the bike bounce slightly. She almost stumbles, but I right her and keep the bike from tipping. My little kitten is not graceful.

"Thank you," she says as I help her with the helmet and set it back on the end of the bike. I got that just for her. I wanted to make sure if she was there, she wouldn't have any excuse not to come back with me tonight.

"You live here?" she asks with slight disbelief. I take a look at the condo and second-guess myself. It's a nice little place, but it's basically a bachelor pad. I mean, it's not huge or in an upscale, gated community, but it's a nice place. A sense of insecurity runs through me. This never fucking happens. But with her it's different. I crave her approval for some unknown reason. If anyone else questions me, my belongings, or anything I do, I shrug it off. I don't give a fuck. But with her, knowing she approves is important to me. I don't think that'll ever change.

She pulls her hair over her shoulders and points over to the dorms behind the condos.

"I live right there," she says as she looks up at me with a small smile. "So you're still the bad boy next door."

I smirk at her and nod my head. Both my shop and my place are close to campus. A lot of business comes from the students. A bike is cheaper than a car.

"I could literally walk back to my place in like two minutes if that fence wasn't there," she says comically. I know right then I need to tell her what's up. I have to give her a chance to go, cause if she stays, she's mine.

"I'll take you back to the dorms if you want. But if you come home with me, I want you, Catherine. I've wanted you for years. And if you walk through that door, I'm not holding back anymore."

"You want me?" she asks with slight disbelief.

"That's putting it mildly, kitten."

"You never--" she starts to say, but doesn't finish.

"I never what?" I ask her, taking a step closer to her. "I never acted on it, no. But I wanted to. Every walk through those woods I thought about stopping and pushing your back against a tree and lifting you up. I wanted to feel that sweet, lush ass of yours in my hands. I dreamed about you wrapping your legs around me while I kissed you and fucked you out there where no one would find us."

Her chest reddens with a blush, and her breathing comes in pants. I see her thighs clench, and I know she's turned on as much as I am.

"But you didn't," she barely whispers.

"I wanted to do that back then, but I couldn't. I want you now though. And there's nothing holding me back. Tell me you want me."

"I want what you want, Ryker." Her whispered words make my dick hard as steel.

I've waited a long time for this.

"Get your ass inside, kitten." Her eyes heat, and she instantly turns on her heels. I smack that cute ass of hers, making her jump.

I'm gonna make sure she doesn't regret this.

Chapter 10

Catherine

I should tell him. I keep thinking over and over that I should tell him I'm a virgin. But I know what he wants, and I know what he'll think.

I can't lie that a part of me has always wanted to wait for him to be my first.

He closes the door to his condo and locks it with a loud click. I turn around, standing in the middle of his living room. Suddenly it becomes all too real. My body tingles with excitement, but also fear. What if I'm not good? What if it's not what I've conjured up in my head?

I start to feel anxious and my nerves threaten to get the best of me, but then he turns around and reaches for his belt.

My pussy clenches with need when I see him unbuckle it and reach for his zipper.

My breaths come in pants as I drop to my knees.

He gives me a sexy grin and walks slowly to me.

I've never done this. But I want to. He shoves his pants down and his dick springs free.

It's so big. Oh my god. That's never going to fit in me. "Open up, kitten," he says as he strokes it. I place my hands on his bare thighs and I stretch my jaw as far as I can. He brushes the hair off my shoulder and pulls it into one hand, gripping at the base of my skull.

"You have no fucking idea how sexy you look right now." I look up at him as he pushes his cock into my mouth. I shield my teeth with my lips and try to push him as far back as I can. I barely get half of him in.

He groans with satisfaction as I push him deeper. I pull back and hollow my cheeks as I bob my head on his cock, each time trying to shove him down deeper and deeper. My eyes burn as I push him down my throat. I try breathing through my nose, but it's hard.

Just as I start thinking I can't do this, Ryker pulls away from me. "Fuck, you feel too good. I'm gonna cum before I'm done with you."

His confession makes me feel a little better. I nervously scoot backward and wipe my lips as daintily as I can as he steps out of his jeans and pulls off his shirt.

My eyes travel along his body. He's a fucking sex god. My panties are practically soaked as he crouches down in front of me and lifts me into his arms.

The movement is sudden, and I let out a small shriek.

"You're wearing too many clothes, kitten." Ryker slips his hand up my shirt and pulls it off of me as he carries me to the bedroom.

My heart beats faster and I try to soothe my nerves by crashing my lips against him.

He moans into my mouth and unclips my bra. I want to hold onto it and cover myself, but I let it fall. It's all or nothing. And I want it all.

He breaks the kiss and drops me on the bed, making me bounce. My arms instinctively cross over my chest. He opens his mouth and I know what he's going to say, but before it comes from his lips, I pull my arms away and let him look at me.

He gives me a wide smile. "Good girl." His eyes travel over my body with appreciation as his deft fingers unbutton my pants and pull them off of me. The rough jeans rub against my ass as I lift my hips and lie there in only my thong. He leans down and pulls my hips to the edge of the bed.

"I've waited too fucking long to taste you." He pushes his thumbs through the thin material, and the sound of the thin lace fabric tearing fills the room.

I close my eyes and lean my head back as he lowers his head to my pussy.

I can't believe this is happening.

He lifts my legs over his shoulders and I feel a cool breeze against my heat. My nipples harden, and part of me wants to hide. Part of me wants to rock my pussy in his face to get off.

He takes a languid lick, and I have to open my eyes to watch. It's so gentle and warm, it's relaxing more than anything at first. But then he flicks his tongue against my clit, and my body bows and jumps at the sensation.

I look up as I hear the sound of him opening a drawer to his nightstand. I let my head fall back as he licks my pussy again and then pulls back to tear the condom wrapper open while he sucks my clit.

A rough chuckle vibrates up his chest as he grips my thighs and pushes me down, sucking my clit into his mouth. My mouth opens wide and my body tries to move away from the sensation. He suctions my clit and pulls back with a *pop*, and the sensation pushes me over the edge. I can't take anymore, and I cum violently. Waves of pleasure crash through my body.

I'm vaguely aware that he's pushing my body up the bed and caging me in. The heat and tingling pleasure rise and fall in slow waves.

"You look so fucking gorgeous when you cum." He cups my right breast and rolls my nipple between his fingers. My body writhes under him. "We gotta work on your control, kitten," he says with a bit of humor as he pinches and pulls my nipple. The slightly painful sensation is directly linked to my clit.

He lowers his lips to my ear as he lines up his cock, nudging the head between my pussy lips and he whispers, "Although I do love how responsive you are."

I barely have a moment to take in his words.

In one hard thrust he's buried deep inside me to the hilt. I feel a sharp pinch and my mouth opens as a silent scream is ripped from my throat and my head flies backward. He stills inside of me and pulls away. He braces himself above me and looks down at me with wide eyes.

I can hardly breathe looking up at him. *He knows.* I turn my head to the side and refuse to look back at him. My pussy hurts, and I just want him to move. But he's not.

A blush heats my cheeks as he grips my chin in his hand and forces me to look at him.

"You're a virgin?" he asks.

I nod my head slowly and swallow thickly. "Not anymore," I finally answer.

His eyes flash with a primal need as he lowers his face to mine and his tongue dives into my mouth. His fingers grip my hips and he moves out of me slowly.

It hurts. My forehead pinches, and I want to move away.

He pushes back in with a hard thrust and grinds his pelvis against my throbbing clit. The pleasure is so strong I have to break our kiss and release a strangled cry.

Fuck, my head thrashes around as my body heats. I feel so full.

He buries his head in the crook of my neck, kissing, licking and biting as he slowly moves in and out of me. His gentle touch is offset by the hard thrusts and his blunt nails digging into my hips.

He nips my earlobe and whispers, "I want to hear you say my name when you cum on my dick," sending a chill down my body and leaving goosebumps along every inch of my skin. Just hearing his dirty words has me on edge.

"Say it," he commands me.

"Ryker." His name falls from my lips instantly. I've dreamed of this a thousand times, but it was never like this. Never this intense and all-consuming.

"That's right, kitten. I'm gonna make you scream my name."

His lips clamp around my nipple and then I feel his teeth. He massages his tongue against the tender skin, and I feel the arousal between my thighs. My head pushes into the mattress as a low, radiating desire moves outward from the pit of my belly, threatening to paralyze my body.

But then he pulls nearly all the way out and I can barely stand it. The pleasure fades and in its place is the hint of pain from his taking my virginity. I need more.

Just as I think it, he slams back into me. His teeth pull against my nipple and I go off. I shatter beneath him. My pussy clamps around his dick, and my body heats with my release. My breathing stops, and I cry out his name.

He lifts himself up again and pushes his thumb against my clit, rubbing slow circles with soft pressure.

Oh, fuck. Yes! It feels so good. My legs wrap around his waist and my heels dig into his ass. I need more.

"Uh-uh," he admonishes me. His rough voice makes my eyes snap to his as he says, "You'll take what I'll give you." I can't reply to him. The only response I can give him is a soft moan as he slams into me again. The force of his touch on my clit makes everything that much better.

The pain slips away as he fucks my body like he owns it, playing with me however he wants.

"Look at me, kitten." My eyes fly to his and he holds my gaze as he pounds into my pussy. My body rocks with each hard thrust, but my eyes stay on his.

His mouth is parted and his eyes half-lidded as he continues his ruthless pace.

The height of my orgasm seems so high. Too

high. I'm going to fall and shatter into a million pieces below him, but he doesn't care. He pushes my thighs farther apart and fucks me deeper, pounding me with a ruthless pace.

"Mine," he growls into my ear as he pinches my clit and I instantly explode under him. A bright white light flashes before my eyes as my body goes numb and then instantly blazes with pleasure.

I scream out his name as my back bows and my pussy spasms around his dick. I feel his thick cock pulsing inside of me as a warmth leaks out of me and drips down my thighs.

He groans in the crook of my neck and whispers my name.

I lie under him trying to catch my breath as he kisses my neck, my jaw and then my lips.

I feel exhausted and sore, wincing as he slowly pulls out of me.

As Ryker climbs off of the bed and heads to the bathroom, I pull the covers up and over my body. Insecurity quickly washes over me as the high of my orgasm dims. I clench my thighs, and the hint of pain makes me feel deliciously used. I don't regret it, not even for a second.

But this is Ryker in real life. Not the man in my dreams. I want more. But I have no idea what he wants.

A pain settles in my chest, and I try to ignore it. To me this is more than what it is to him. I can't hold that against him though. I got what I wanted. And I got what I asked for.

I finally got the bad boy experience I knew Ryker would give me. And he has the piece of me I've always wanted to give him.

All I can think as I hear him turn on the faucet to the shower is, *Now what?*

Chapter 11

Ryker

I walk back into the bedroom with the warm cloth and look at the tinge of pink on it.

She waited for me. Never in a million years would I have thought she'd do that.

She's mine for good now. She's mine. I have an odd sense of pride that I can't let go of. I was her first.

As I walk back to her with a grin on my face, it falls. I stop to take a good look at her. She's got the covers wrapped tight around her, and she's not looking at me.

I don't know what's going on in that pretty little head of hers. But I'm not letting her go. It's not happening.

Whatever's going on, I'm making sure she knows I

want her.

I climb onto the bed and pull the covers back. Her eyes widen and fly to mine. I can feel them on me, but I ignore her. "Spread your legs for me."

My dick jumps as she obeys my command. I see her wince with pain though, and I don't like that. I tried not to be too rough on her, but I lost control a bit.

I gently wipe the pink-tinged cum from her legs and ass. A bit's gotten onto the sheets, too. Her little pussy is swollen and red. I watch her face as I gently wipe the cloth against her sensitive flesh.

She closes her eyes, but it's a look of comfort. Good. I push her thighs closed and get off the bed enough to toss the washcloth into the hamper. The sheets will need to be washed too, but it can wait.

I lie down under the comforter and pull her body into mine. She's a little stiff, and I don't like that. She's feeling insecure. I don't want that for her.

"What's wrong, Catherine?" I ask her in a soft voice. "Did I hurt you?" I already know I did. It was her first time. I know she's going to be sore.

Her body relaxes some as she gently shakes her head and replies, "No, it felt good." Just good? She felt like fucking heaven. I knew she would feel like that. She tacks on, "Really good," and a small smile plays at her lips.

"What's bothering you, kitten?" I nudge her chin

with the tip of my nose, and she turns in my arms to finally look at me.

"I'm scared." Her confession puts my guard on high alert. Whatever her worry is, I'll ease it for her.

"Tell me why," I say and keep her gaze, willing her to tell me the truth.

"I don't know what this is." Her voice cracks, and it breaks my heart that she's so insecure. I can't blame her. I fucking jumped on her the second I got her back here. It was selfish of me. I run my thumb along her bottom lip and think about what I should tell her.

I finally settle on the truth. "It's whatever you want it to be." I'll take whatever she's willing to give me. Maybe that makes me pussy-whipped. But I don't care. I just want her.

"Do you want me still?" she asks with a pained voice, and her eyes shining with vulnerability.

A soft smile turns my lips up and I lean down to kiss the tip of her nose. "I finally got a taste of you, I'm not letting go now."

"What if I want more than just sex?" she asks while looking down at the comforter and picking at nonexistent loose threads. Relief flows through me.

"That's what you're worried about?" I ask her, cupping her chin and tilting her face so she has to look at me.

"I--" she starts to say something, but then she moves

her head out of my grip and looks away as she haltingly says, "I think I've loved you for a long time, Ryker."

My heartbeat slows, and my skin heats. I don't use that word, *love*. I don't believe in it. One minute my parents loved me, and the next they hated me. I know I need to say something to her to ease her worries, but I don't believe in that word. I splay my hand across her belly and pull her small body closer to mine. I kiss the crook of her neck gently. "I've wanted you for years, Catherine. Not just in my bed and screaming my name. But I wanted you next to me. I wanted to be good enough for you. I wanted to be the man who deserved to have you." She looks up at me with her big doe eyes like she doesn't believe me, but it's true. Every word. "I don't know that I am right now. But I'm working hard to be that man, and I want you. Not just for tonight, and not just for sex. I want you to be mine. Period."

She surprises me as she takes my face in her hands and kisses me with a passion I wasn't expecting. It's a sweet kiss, but there's more to it than that. It's like all restraint has left her. There's nothing holding us back.

I pull away just slightly and nip her bottom lip. I look into her eyes and see nothing but happiness. That's better. I want her to be happy.

I let out a yawn and almost tell her to go to sleep, but then a thought pops into my head.

"How are you gonna tell your father?" I ask her. That worries me. Her father never liked me. Not that many parents did back then. And not that I could blame him.

She giggles. "He's gonna have a fucking heart attack. But he'll get over it."

"You think it'll be that easy, huh?" I'm not looking forward to that family dinner. My heart clenches in my chest. I can't split her up from her parents. They were good to her, and they were right to keep me away from her. I don't want to keep her from having something that I'm missing out on.

"I'm all grown up now, Ryker," she says with a hint of humor. "Besides, you should've seen my last boyfriend."

My body goes tense. I don't like the thought of her with someone else. "I'm kidding!" she says with a wide smile before nuzzling into my chest.

I let my body relax and run my hand down her side. My fingers trail along her skin and give her the shivers. I let out a small chuckle.

"Dad might never approve, but he'll get over it." I nod once at her words. That's true. And I'll do my best to show them I've changed. "What matters is that I want you."

I smile at her words. That pride fills my chest again.

It's a feeling I don't get often, and I want it every day from here on out.

"You have no idea how much I wanted you," she confesses. But I do. I knew she wanted me, but back then it wouldn't have been good for her. I wouldn't have been good for her.

I huff a laugh. "Well I've got a hold on you now, kitten." I kiss the tip of her nose. "And I'm not gonna let go."

Epilogue

Ryker

Two Years Later

I'm so damn nervous. I hate this feeling. I wipe my hands off with a towel and make sure all the muck's gone. Mr. Parker's gonna be here soon. Usually I'm proud looking at my choppers when they're all done. I look over the bike and love it. The design is hot. The chrome is shiny, and the leather smooth. Everything's perfect.

But it's for Catherine's father. Mr. Parker's approval makes me nervous.

I know I make my kitten happy now. There's no doubt in my mind. But her father's a different story.

Ever since that night at the party, she's been staying

with me. That's how I want it. I need her in my bed and cumming on my dick every night. That's the way it should be. Even though Khloe got kicked out of school for public drunkenness, I wouldn't let her go back to the dorms. Catherine's my girl, she should be in my bed.

But I've also been going to their family dinners every other Sunday. And that's... fucking exhausting. It's getting better though. I can at least admit that.

At first I refused to go. Who the hell wants to go to their girlfriend's parents' house? Especially since I know her father, and I remember how he told me to stay away from her. It was years ago, but still.

It made her so upset though. So I caved and went with her to her parents' house. My parents aren't next door anymore. It's odd seeing the house I grew up in. It looks different. New siding, and the current owners painted the shutters. They fixed the fence out back and put in large bushes on the edge of the sidewalk. It doesn't look like the place I grew up. Which is a good thing in a lot of ways.

It sucked being there that first day though. I haven't seen my parents in years. Not since they lost the house and came to me for money. That ended real quick when I told them no. I could see the look in my father's eyes. That same mean look he used to give me before the fights would start. But I didn't back down. If they want a relationship with me, they can have one. But if they just want money they'll have to go somewhere else.

It hurts still that they left and never came back, but it's for the best.

My parents are nothing like the Parkers.

Catherine was blessed with parents who really love her. They love her enough to be concerned about the fact that we're seeing each other, too.

They know she isn't at the dorms, which only makes it more awkward. That first night her father looked at me the way a man looks at the prick who's fucking his daughter. Can't blame him for it, but it didn't make spaghetti Sunday go by any quicker.

I had to grin when I overheard Catherine's mother scolding him in the kitchen. Janette reminds me a lot of Catherine. But there's no doubt I'm nothing like George.

Although he did order a custom build from me. So that means something. That, and he didn't put up much fuss when we told them we're buying a new house closer in town when Catherine graduates this semester. So those are good signs.

"Hey! You aren't dressed!" I hear my kitten come into the garage and practically stomp her little foot.

I turn around and smile at her. I've got a wrench in one hand and a towel in the other and say, "I'm going as a mechanic."

She rolls her eyes and walks down the two steps so she's on the concrete slab. "You gotta hurry, babe. As soon as Daddy leaves we need to get going, or we're going to be late!"

She's excited to see everyone from the party. Like it's a reunion of sorts. As if we even stayed that long last time.

I hope Jake and Levi have another bet going, 'cause this time I am fucking her somewhere in that house. With that cute little skirt and fishnets, fuck yeah I'm getting in that pussy as soon as we find an empty room.

My dick twitches, and I think about taking her ass up to the office real quick, but then I hear a car pull up.

If her father doesn't hate me now, he sure as hell would if he walked in on me fucking his baby girl.

I try to think of everything I can to get this erection down as Catherine walks over to her old man. He steps out of the car and looks back at me with a tight smile.

"You're going to love it!" Catherine squeals, pulling on his arm before he's even had the chance to shut his car door. He kicks it closed and keeps up with her pace as he comes into the garage.

"Mr. Parker," I greet him and put down the wrench and towel.

"I told you to call me George," he says.

Catherine rolls her eyes and says, "And I told you to call him Dad." I cock a brow at her. My little kitten is cute and sweet, but we're both giving her a look to tell her she needs to get over that wish. It's not happening.

Her father walks around the bike and I square my shoulders. It's exactly what he asked for, and then some. I'm confident in my work, and I'm damn good at what I do, but I still want him to like it.

He nods his head and smiles. "She's a beauty. Good work," he says proudly.

Catherine rocks on her heels with glee. "Told you."

I nod my head once and say simply, "Glad you like it." But that's an understatement.

"Mikey's in reception today; he can take that last payment there if you still insist on paying." I wanted to do it for free. After all, he's my girl's father. And I've got enough business that I'm not at a loss. But he's been persistent.

"I know where it is," he says with a smile.

"I'm getting a Coke," Catherine says, absentmindedly walking over to the vending machine. I swear she uses the machines more than the guys do.

I watch her walk easily across the garage and my eyes wander to that ass of hers. I want her today just as much as I did when I first met her, maybe even more.

"Walk with me, Ryker," her father says as he heads up the stairs to the receptionist's area inside the shop attached to the garage. I nod my head and walk behind him.

As soon as we're inside the building, he stops and turns to face me.

"It's been two years, hasn't it?" George asks me.

"Two years?"

"Since you and Catherine started," he waves his hand in front of him and purses his lips trying to think up the right word.

"Dating?" I offer. Although what we have is so much more than that. She's my everything, and I'm the same to her.

"Sure," he says as he turns to face me with his brow furrowed. "What I'm getting at is the fact her finger doesn't have a ring on it." My fingers itch to reach into my pocket. I just got one last week. He doesn't know, but I'm proposing tonight. My heart swells, and pride runs through me.

"Is that your blessing, George?" I ask him.

"It's the best you're gonna get, son." I nod my head and start to tell him my intention, but Catherine opens the door. I look over my shoulder and see her narrow her eyes as she says, "You two having a pow wow?" she asks.

Her father chuckles and says, "Just headed in now, sweetie."

He walks off down the hall and I turn to face Catherine. I'm gonna marry this woman. I'm a lucky man.

"What were you two talking about?" she asks

suspiciously.

"None of your business." I hold her gaze as she clucks her tongue. She's deciding if she wants to push, but I know she won't.

She sighs and crosses her arms. "Are you gonna get dressed now at least?"

"Yeah, I'm heading back now."

We're going as school girl and professor tonight. Catherine's choice.

I kiss the tip of her nose. "I love you, kitten." She's showed me over the years what those words really mean, and I really do love her.

"I love you too," she begins in a peppy voice, "but I'm gonna kick your ass if you don't get dressed."

I smirk down at her and make sure her father's out of sight so I can pinch her ass. She squeals and jumps.

"Watch that mouth of yours," I warn her like I always do. "It's gonna get you into trouble."

She winks at me and saunters off, trying to be sexy, which she is. "I'm counting on it."

Thank you for reading these sexy novellas, intense shorts, and some of my favorite stories I've written. I usually don't write quickies, but I have to admit I love these stories and the road they paved to lead me where I am today in this writing career. Thank you for making it all possible.

Happy reading and best wishes,

Willow xx

About the Author

Thank you so much for reading my romances. I'm just a stay at home Mom and an avid reader turned Author and I couldn't be happier.

I hope you love my books as much as I do!

More by Willow Winters
www.willowwinterswrites.com/books

Made in the USA
Middletown, DE
26 January 2025